If You Enjoy This Book,
Check Out Phil's
Sixth-Grade Adventures in:

THE RULES OF NEVER

THE RULES OF NEVER: YEAR TWO

A Middle School Survival Guide

By

Phil Adam

ISBN: 9798740880365

To Clara, Caden and Jenna

Acknowledgements

I wish to thank the following individuals who were helpful in the production of this book: Caden Adam, Tara Adam, Nicole Adam-Nelson, Carter Dziatkewich, Paul Hering and Den Persick for their input; Bill Gilbert, Kim Dziatkewich, Clara Nelson and Bill Nelson for their suggestions; Carolyn Paplham for her illustrations and cover design; early-draft readers Donna Jahnke and Lin Persick; Steve Frozena and Bill Wheeler for their assistance in editing and proofreading and Den Persick for his help in layout, design and publishing. And finally, my wife, Ellen, for her support and encouragement.

CONTENTS

PROLOGUE

I set aside the *Lost Creek Middle School Rules of Conduct* and turned off my bedside lamp. I lay in bed, wide awake and sweating, and for the umpteenth time checked the clock:10:13 PM. In nine hours and thirty-seven minutes, seventh grade would begin.

A year ago at this time, I had gone through the same ordeal. Same rules of conduct. Same bed. Same wide-awake-with-beads-of-sweat state. Same worries.

What happens if I come across something the rules don't cover?

I had a right to worry. Last year I ended up learning many lessons the hard way, so I had to make my own rules as I went along. Rules like Never Eat Chili the Night before School and Never Yell at a Kid Named Moose. I recorded these and other experiences in a notebook called THE RULES OF NEVER.

Wait a minute. That's it!

I flicked the lamp back on, bolted from my bed and rummaged through my backpack. I found what I was looking for—a blank notebook and marker—and scribbled THE RULES OF NEVER: YEAR TWO on the cover. I stowed the notebook and marker in my desk drawer.

With a sigh of relief, I hopped back into bed, switched off the lamp and settled in for a good night's sleep. *Now* I was ready for seventh grade.

Or *was* I?

NEVER FORGET THE MODEL STUDENT STRATEGY

Front row. Seats closest to the teacher. Worst seats in class.

Most teachers sit students in alphabetical order by last name. With a surname of Abrams, I was toast the minute I walked through the classroom door.

For five of my six years in grade school and my first year of middle school, teachers assigned me seat one in row one.

Often, I sat directly in front of the teacher's desk. This ruled out chatting with classmates, fooling around or finishing work due in a later class.

The location also kept me from texting or reading my messages. And forget about doodling, chewing gum or daydreaming.

The only time I didn't sit in the front row was fourth grade. That year Mrs. Ginn reversed the order. She assigned Grayson Zimmer seat one and me the last desk in the back row.

Sitting in the back of the room was like being invisible. If I didn't cough, sneeze, burp or raise my hand, Mrs. Ginn ignored me.

Rarely did I recite a poem or read a paragraph out loud. I hardly ever solved a math problem on the whiteboard or predicted science outcomes. I seldom answered questions about a story the class had read or defined social studies terms. I loved it.

Unfortunately, sitting in the best seat in class lasted only two months. In late October, Oliver, who sat right in front of me, squeezed out a big, smelly fart that filled the back of the room like a dense fog. The putrid odor called for evasive measures, but everyone was stuck in a desk.

Instead, a buzz of conversation started among the kids sitting around Oliver. The noise drew the attention of Mrs. Ginn, who was writing a math problem on the whiteboard.

The teacher whirled around and faced the class. "What's going on back there?"

Except for a faint giggle here and there, we all sat in silence.

Mrs. Ginn slammed her dry-erase marker on her desk and marched toward the back of the room. Halfway down my aisle, Oliver's stink bomb stopped the teacher dead in her tracks.

Waving her hand in front of her round face like a windshield wiper in a thunderstorm, Mrs. Ginn searched for the culprit. As she scanned the back rows, I held my hand over my mouth to hide my grin.

Everyone looked innocent, so Mrs. Ginn turned to walk back to the front of the room. That's when she saw me snatching a paper airplane off the floor.

I could tell by Mrs. Ginn's angry scowl she deemed playing with a paper airplane in class a major offense. "Phil, get your books and switch seats with Grayson," she snapped, still fanning the air with her hand.

Seconds later, I found myself sitting in the first seat in row one, right across from the teacher's desk.

√   √   √

Tired of sitting in the first seat in the first row, I hoped my seventh-grade teachers would let students sit where they wanted.

Hope faded when my parents received a letter from Lost Creek Middle School a week before school started. The letter welcomed me to Lost Creek and listed my teachers and my class schedule.

I had the dreadful Ms. Joyner for homeroom and English and the horrid Mr. Fry for health. Since I had both teachers in sixth grade and they sat students by last name, I assumed they would follow the same routine in seventh.

I didn't know if my other teachers assigned seats, but my dream of sitting where I wanted looked bleak.

However, I felt better after Shane Olson and Caden Jacobs, my best buds, texted me. Both had Ms. Joyner for homeroom, so the three of us followed the same class schedule.

Seven days later school began.

Ms. Joyner sat at her desk studying a sheet of paper while my classmates and I filed into first-hour English. "Take a seat and get ready for announcements," she said in a firm voice without looking up.

I strolled across the front of the room searching for Caden and Shane. Instead, I spotted Clara Pearson motioning for me to sit next to her. I had met Clara during the summer at a state park when our parents set up campsites next to each other.

What first struck me about Clara was her height and weight. She stood almost six feet and was so skinny a gust of wind might bend her in half. Outgoing and friendly, she spent seven days hanging out with me. We had a blast swimming, biking and tubing.

During that week, I discovered Clara and I had a lot in common. Both of us were going to be seventh graders at Lost Creek, rooted for the Green Bay Packers and watched sci-fi movies.

Not spotting CJ or Shane, I headed down the aisle toward Clara.

"Hey, Clara," I said, stashing my notebook under the desk across from her. "Long time, no see."

"Yeah, you too, Phil."

As I eased into the desk, I noticed Clara's school supplies. On her desk lay two binders, each with spiral notebooks inside. A stack of index cards, three No. 2 pencils, a blue pen and a highlighter lay neatly atop the binders.

I peered at Clara. "Seriously?"

"What?"

"Two binders?"

Clara tucked a stray strand of her fiery red hair behind her ear. "One binder is for first and second hour, and the other is for third and fourth."

"I suppose you have another binder in your locker for your afternoon classes."

"Of course."

I shook my head. "It's the first day."

"I want to be prepared."

"You're joking, right?"

"Nope." Clara drummed her long fingers on her

desk. "Can't wait to get going."

"Obviously, you didn't have Joyner last year."

"No. Why?"

"Cuz, if you did, you wouldn't be so keen to get started."

"It can't be that bad." Clara's voice sank almost to a whisper.

"You'll see," I said under my breath. "She has the charm of a cobra and the personality of a mannequin."

Clara pressed her hand against her mouth to suppress a giggle.

"No more talking," the teacher announced, raising her voice to get everybody's attention.

Moments later, the PA on the front wall burst to life. "Good morning everyone, and welcome to Lost Creek Middle School, home of the Fighting Frogs. I'm Principal Knox." His voice echoed through the room. "I hope you had a fabulous summer."

The principal paused for a few seconds. "First, some terrific news. Starting Monday, morning announcements will be broadcast over closed-circuit television."

"Great," I grumbled to Clara. "Listening to announcements is bad enough, now I have to watch them too."

"Sounds exciting," Clara said in a low voice.

"You can't be serious?"

"I'm kidding," Clara whispered.

"Oh," I whispered back.

Principal Knox babbled on. "I have a number of announcements, so put on your listening ears."

That was my cue to stop paying attention. I propped my chin in my palms and watched a fly bump against the windowpane, seeking a way out.

While following the fly from window to window, I noticed the kids sitting in the back rows. Some were leaning forward in their desks with arms crossed and heads resting on their arms, trying to catch some Zs. Others doodled, stared at a wall or played with their phones.

In the back row sat Brook Bader, one of the cutest girls in school. With the last name of Bader, she'd sit right behind me in most of my classes.

Things were looking up.

Principal Knox droned on, but he caught my attention when he said, "Enough from me. Let's make this year your best ever. Go Frogs."

After announcements, Ms. Joyner let out a heavy sigh. She picked up the sheet of paper she had been busily studying, pushed herself away from her desk and stood.

"Kids in back can wake up now." Ms. Joyner's voice rose with each word. "Today will be the last time anyone doesn't listen to announcements."

The teacher plodded to the lectern and draped herself over it. "I'm Ms. Joyner. Welcome to homeroom and English."

She sounded as if she hadn't slept in days.

Ms. Joyner yawned. "To make it easier for me to learn your names and take attendance, I drew up a seating chart. When I call your name, sit in the desk I direct you to."

My eyes drifted upward to the ceiling. I knew what came next.

Ms. Joyner glanced at the sheet of paper she clutched in her left hand. "Phil Abrams."

I grudgingly raised my hand.

"Nice to see you again, Mister Abrams."

That makes one of us.

"You sit there," Ms. Joyner commanded. She gestured toward the first seat in row one across from her desk.

"Here we go again," I mumbled to myself.

"Have a great day, Sunshine." Clara waved a tiny goodbye and flashed me a bright smile.

I stuck my tongue out at her.

Clara made a pouty face and giggled.

I picked up my notebook, dragged myself from the desk and halfheartedly stood.

"We don't have all day, Mister Abrams," Ms. Joyner barked as I dawdled to my seat.

"I do," I said a little too loudly.

"Well, you're making a great first impression, Abrams." Ms. Joyner glared at me like my father does when I fart in church.

I slapped my notebook on the desk, slid into my seat and sighed. At least Brook would be sitting right behind me.

"Zoey Appleberry," Ms. Joyner announced.

Say what? Who's Zoey Appleberry?

I glanced up as a short, nerdy-looking girl strolled toward me. Her hair hung down in two long braided pigtails, and thick bangs covered her forehead. Two tiny moles dotted her left cheek.

As Zoey approached my desk she flashed me a smile, revealing a mouthful of metal. She slipped into the desk behind me.

"Brook Bader," Ms. Joyner called out.

Figures.

I sat and stared at a blank chalkboard on the side wall as Ms. Joyner continued assigning seats.

"Jennifer Davis." I turned to see Jennifer pick up her binder and stand. "Jennifer, you sit here." The teacher pointed to the desk across from mine.

This can't be happening.

Davis, a brainiac, was one of the most obnoxious kids at Lost Creek. A total pain in the butt, she made a scene in the cafeteria at least once a month. An outspoken vegan, she objected to kids eating anything that once had a face.

Last year, Davis wore black clothes and black tennis shoes every day. She even painted her long fingernails black. Her jet-black hair with a red streak was usually pulled behind her head in a ponytail and tied with a black ribbon.

Today was no exception.

Davis plopped her binder and pens on her desk and slithered into her seat. The expression on her egg-shaped face made it clear she was unhappy sitting by a guy once nicknamed "Stinky Pants."

She removed her rectangular-framed glasses resting on her turned-up nose and set them on her binder, knocking a pen on the floor.

Davis leaned toward me. "I don't EVER wanna talk to you, Dorkenstein," she muttered in her irritating scratchy voice. Davis bent over and snatched up the pen that had rolled off her desk. "And if you fart, I'll have you arrested."

"If I fart, I guarantee you'll be the first to know," I muttered back and grinned.

Davis shot me a disgusted look.

After assigning seats, Ms. Joyner returned to her desk and handed out textbooks and Chromebooks. When students had both, she addressed the class. "You are responsible for the care of your textbook and Chromebook."

The teacher stood and went on with her sermon. "Losing or damaging either of them will result in a fee that must be paid before you receive your final report card."

Ms. Joyner stepped over to the whiteboard and snatched a long wooden ruler from the tray. She ambled over to a couple of king-sized bulletin boards on the front wall.

One bulletin board had Angry Verbs printed in fat purple letters surrounded by words like: smashed, ripped, flattened and walloped.

The other board had Classroom Expectations printed in large lime letters centered on top. Eleven were listed under the heading in no particular order.

Standing between the two bulletin boards, Ms. Joyner shoved her glasses firmly into place. "Let's begin today's lesson by reading together classroom expectations."

Using a ruler for a pointer, she slapped Expectation One. "Be on Time," the class said in unison.

What are we, in kindergarten?

I stifled a yawn with the back of my hand, slouched

down in the desk and closed my eyes. They snapped open when Ms. Joyner thundered, "Mister Abrams, Expectation Four is Stay Alert in Class. Wake up, you may learn something."

"Come to English Prepared," classmates and I recited together.

After we read the eleventh expectation, Ms. Joyner plodded over to a table and grabbed a handful of papers. Facing the class, she held a sheet above her head. "This is a twenty-word spelling list. You will be tested on these tomorrow." She passed them out.

Joyner, the worst seat in class, no Bader but a Davis and a spelling test. Seventh grade was off to a great start—NOT!

As Ms. Joyner placed the extra sheets on her desk, the bell rang signaling the end of class. Twenty-three students rushed past the teacher, herded through the door and poured into the hallway.

I waited for Clara. By the time she gathered her materials, everyone else had left. We walked out the door together and merged into a sea of noisy seventh graders.

Shane and Caden stood across the hallway by a drinking fountain, waiting for me. "First day of school, Abrams, and you already have a girlfriend," Shane hollered. "Can't leave you alone for a minute."

"Give it a rest, Shane," I shouted back.

"You're the one flirting, Abrams," Shane teased. "Don't yell at me."

"Don't mind him, Clara," I said. "Shane's got a big mouth."

Clara and I made our way to the drinking fountain, where I introduced Clara to my friends.

"Clara, this windbag is Shane Olson. Shane, meet Clara Pearson."

"Hey, Clara, and don't believe a word Phil says."

"Hi, Shane." Clara gave him a pleasant smile.

"What about me, Phil?" Caden joked.

"Clara, this ugly guy is Caden Jacobs."

"Hi, Clara. Friends call me CJ. And Phil, have you looked in the mirror lately?"

Clara chuckled. "Nice to meet you, CJ."

Shane cut in. "I don't wanna be rude, but I need to go the office."

"What didya do now?" I asked.

"Ha-ha. If you must know, Phil, I hafta turn in my physical for basketball."

Shane swung around to leave. "C'mon, CJ. We gotta go. Otherwise we'll be late for science."

"Chill, Shane," CJ said. "Let's go after second hour."

"Fine." Shane shot CJ an irritated look.

The four of us set off for class.

After science, CJ and Shane headed to the office, while Clara and I wove our way through the crowded hallway to social studies.

"Well, I'm zero for two," I told Clara.

"What does that supposed to mean?"

"In my first two classes, I'm sitting in my usual spot, the first seat in row one."

Clara snagged my arm and stopped, a concerned expression on her face. "Does sitting in the front row bother you that much? You're such a baby, Phil. You're making a big deal out of nothing. You don't always have to sit in front."

"Whaddaya mean? If a teacher has a seating chart, I end up in the first desk in the first row."

"All teachers make seating charts, but not every teacher sits kids by last name. My older brother, Jackson, told me our social studies teacher, Mrs. Ward, waits a week before assigning seats."

"How does that help me?"

"It's not by last name." We stopped in front of Clara's locker.

"With my luck, she'd still assign me the first seat."

"Not if you use the Model Student Strategy." Clara spun the dial on her combination lock to clear it.

"The what?"

"The Model Student Strategy."

Clara entered her combination, lifted the latch and jerked open her locker. "Jackson taught me the strategy in fifth grade. I usually don't care where I sit, but if the teacher doesn't sit kids by last name and you want to be in back, I'd try it. Last year, I sat in back in math."

"How does the strategy work?" I asked, now intrigued.

"During the first week, the teacher gets to know the students and each day records where they sit. Most students, when given a choice, sit with their friends in the same area of the room day after day."

Clara set her binder on the shelf and continued explaining the strategy. "After a week, the teacher has a record of who sat in front, the faces parked in the middle and the kids seated in back."

"Let's motor," I told Clara. "We can talk on the way to class."

"What's the rush?" Clara gently closed her locker and faced me.

"Look at the time. We're gonna be late."

Clara glimpsed at the large hallway clock. "Phil, you're such a worrywart. Lighten up. We have eighteen seconds. Plus teachers never give tardy slips the first day of school."

"Yeah, I know. I just like being on time."

Clara explained the rest of the strategy on the way to social studies. "Today sit in the front row and not by CJ and Shane. Show an interest in class, take part in discussions and hand in assignments on time. Do this until the seating chart comes out."

"That'll be hard to do," I said.

"If you want a crack at sitting in back of the room instead of whining about having to sit in front, you'll try this. No promises, but why not give it a shot? I'm going to."

"You're dreaming, Clara. Know what? I'll bet you a slice of pizza from a la carte your scheme doesn't work."

"You're on."

We strolled into social studies.

Two seats in the front row remained empty. Since I had nothing to lose except some pizza, I followed Clara's suggestion. I parked myself in one of the vacant desks. On my left sat a girl I knew from sixth grade. On my right sat a girl I had never seen before.

Clara grabbed my usual seat, directly across from the teacher's desk. Shane and CJ, on the other hand, planted themselves in back.

After class, I waited for Shane and CJ in the hallway.

"I don't believe you, Phil," CJ said as he walked toward me. "You're totally hopeless."

"Whaddaya talking about?"

"You hate sitting in front," CJ said. "You can sit anywhere in the room before we're assigned seats, and you plunk yourself down fifteen feet from the teacher's desk."

"I'm trying the Model Student game plan."

"The *what?*" Shane asked.

"I'll explain at lunch."

Shane and CJ exchanged puzzled glances as the three of us headed off to computer science.

At lunch, I spelled out Clara's Model Student Strategy to Shane and CJ between bites of my peanut butter and banana sandwich. When I was through explaining, Shane stared at my forehead until I said, "Whaddaya looking at?"

"Checking if you have a screw loose, because that's the dumbest idea I've ever heard."

"Yeah, Phil. You've finally lost it," CJ added.

"Funny, guys, but before either of you say anything else stupid, wait until Mrs. Ward assigns us seats." I noisily drained the rest of my juice box.

My friends promised not to bring up the strategy again until the seating chart came out.

For the first five days in social studies, I did what Clara suggested. I took a seat in the front row and earned an A or B on my assignments. I paid attention and added a few tidbits to class discussion.

The next week, Mrs. Ward unveiled her seating chart. Kids who had sat in front found themselves in back. Students who had taken a seat in back were now stuck in front. Friends sat across the room from one another. I was parked in the back row across from Clara.

After taking our seats, Clara eyeballed me and mouthed, "You owe me a slice of pizza."

"I know," I mouthed back. I had lost the bet, but it was a small price to pay for a great seat.

After class Shane and CJ, both of whom now sat in the front third of the room, waited for me in the hallway. "Tell us again about your Model Student Strategy," Shane said, as the three of us headed down the corridor toward the computer lab.

A smug smile spread across my face. "You're gonna have to wait till lunch, and it's gonna cost both of you a slice of pizza from a la carte." I chuckled, knowing one slice would go toward paying off Clara's bet.

After studying for my spelling test that night, I thought about the Model Student Strategy and how it had worked like a charm. However, with the exception of PE, band, computer science and social studies, I still sat in the first seat, first row in all my classes.

I hated sitting in the first seat, but I couldn't do anything about it. Having my parents change our last name to Zingle was out of the question, so I played a mental game of names.

If an Aaron family moved into town with a seventh grader who was placed in my homeroom, I'd move back one seat. And if the Aaron family had twins—that would move me two seats back.

What kinds of names, and how many new kids, would it take to get me to the back row?

Candace Aardvark, where are you when I need you?

RULE TWO

NEVER FART IN ENGLISH

"Come on, Phil. Get up," Dad said loudly, shaking me awake.

"Five more minutes." I pulled my pillow over my face.

"You're already behind schedule. Didn't you set your alarm?"

"Must've forgot," I mumbled.

"Let's get moving, Phil," my father said as he left the room.

I tossed the pillow aside, rubbed the sleep from my eyes and scrambled out of bed. After a quick shower,

I got ready for school, slung my backpack over my shoulder and dashed downstairs. Kaylee, my annoying ten-year-old sister, sat at the kitchen table spooning her Cheerios.

"Oversleep again?" she asked between spoonfuls.

"Why do you care?"

"I don't."

"Then why ask?"

"Cut it out, you two," Mom barked.

I dumped my backpack beside the counter and snatched a leftover bean burrito and a jug of orange juice from the fridge. I took a seat across from Kaylee and poured myself a glass of OJ. I inhaled the burrito and chugged the juice.

I checked my phone for the time. Five minutes to catch the bus. I returned the jug to the fridge, set my glass in the dishwasher and chucked the burrito wrapper in the garbage.

"Gotta go, Mom." I scooped up my backpack, put on a jacket and belched.

"Phil!" Mom gave me a stern look.

"Excuse me." I slipped on my backpack and dashed out the back door.

I took off at a dead run for the bus stop and when I arrived, kids were almost done boarding. I stood at the end of a short line and caught my breath. Seconds later I climbed the steps onto the bus.

"Phil, over here," CJ shouted, waving his hand.

I moseyed down the aisle, slipped off my backpack and plopped down alongside CJ.

"Sorry for not waiting." CJ stuffed his phone in his pocket. "Didn't think you were coming."

"Overslept. Forgot to set my alarm."

A short time later, CJ and I arrived at school. "Hope my day goes better than it started," I told CJ as we weaved our way through the bustling crowded hallway.

I stopped at my locker, grabbed my English materials and my Chromebook and made my way to homeroom.

I sat at my desk tapping my front teeth with a pencil, waiting for announcements.

Suddenly, Principal Knox appeared on the TV in front of the room. "Good morning, fellow Frogs. Today is Tuesday, October 13. Make sure to wish Mr. Ash, our custodian, a happy birthday."

The principal rested his arms on the table in front of him and leaned forward. "A reminder to teachers: With Friday being a teacher workday, next week's lesson plans are due Thursday. Now here's Ellen, your Student Council vice president, to tell you what's happening at Lost Creek."

Boy, Ellen's even prettier than Brook Bader.

"Thank you, Principal Knox," Ellen said. "Today's

lunch menu is hot dogs or veggie burger, fries or salad, baked beans and mixed fruit."

Ellen brushed back strands of her hair with the back of her wrist. "The eighth-grade football team plays Franklin at home at 4:00. The girls' volleyball team has a match at Parkview Middle School at 4:15. Photography Club will meet in the library rather than the art room."

Ellen held up a large, eye-catching poster with kids dancing. "Don't forget Friday's dance in the gym. The dance starts at 7:00 and ends at 9:30. The theme is 'Dance for a Cause.'"

Ellen laid the poster on the table. "Tickets cost a dollar and can be purchased at the bookstore during lunch. Ticket sales benefit the local Humane Society. This concludes today's announcements. Have a fantastic day."

Impossible when the day begins with Joyner.

Ms. Joyner, the worst English teacher ever had taught at Lost Creek for the past sixteen years. I looked forward to her class as much a plate of Mom's grilled brussels sprouts sprinkled with crumbled goat cheese.

In her late thirties, Ms. Joyner usually reeked of perfume that smelled like a grilled cheese sandwich. On most days she wore lipstick the color of an overripe plum and violet eyeshadow. Every now and then I caught a glimpse of a tiny red heart tattoo on the back of her neck.

Fit and toned, the teacher's upper arms resembled a weightlifter's. Rumors floated around school she had been a member of a college rowing team.

I had no idea why Ms. Joyner disliked me, but I knew why my friends and I disliked her. She bored students to death, treated everyone unfairly and shamed kids in class.

Ms. Joyner did, however, have one remarkable trait. Due to a snout resembling a badger, she had a keen sense of smell.

Older students had warned me about Ms. Joyner's unique ability, but Clara's brother summed it up best: "Joyner is like a police sniffer dog in human form. If you cut one in English, she'll catch you."

How exceptional was Ms. Joyner's sense of smell? She could sniff out:

- smelly socks lying in a closed locker
- the flavor of gum a kid was chewing
- what students ate for breakfast
- the deodorant brand a kid was wearing

Most amazing of all, Ms. Joyner could detect the teensiest fart. But detection wasn't the sole problem students faced. The teacher also had the uncanny knack of pinpointing where in the room the fart came from.

I'll never forget the day Ms. Joyner caught me.

The class quietly worked on an end-of-chapter assignment on pronouns. While writing the answer to question four, my pencil lead broke.

I eased out of my desk and strolled over to the pencil sharpener mounted on a bookcase in the room's back corner.

I stuck the pencil into the sharpener and rapidly cranked the handle. I don't know if it was the sharpener's grinding sound or the bean burrito I scarfed down for breakfast, but I had a sudden urge to fart.

I glanced at the clock above the glossy whiteboard in front of the room: 8:44. Eleven minutes remained in class. If I held the gas until the bell rang, the hallway would be teeming with seventh graders. I could then pin the blame on someone else.

My first thought was to return to my desk since it's easier to hold a fart sitting than standing. But if I ripped one walking to my seat, the class and Ms. Joyner would hear the blast. The explosion might also cause a temporary hearing loss to nearby classmates.

Instead, I resharpened my pencil while trying to relieve the pressure in my gut. First, I stood erect, shoulders back, like a soldier at attention, but that didn't work.

Next, I transferred my weight from one foot to the other, which had no effect either. As a last resort, I squeezed my butt cheeks together, which helped a little.

I checked the time. Over nine and a half minutes remained in class. Sharpening my pencil for that length of time would draw attention. And squeezing my butt cheeks for that long was impossible.

I quickly surveyed the room. Classmates worked on their assignments, and Ms. Joyner sat at her desk grading papers. No one paid me the slightest bit of attention.

Ms. Joyner's desk was located in one corner of the room. I stood in the corner crosswise from her desk, about forty feet away. If I passed a tiny amount of gas, she might not smell it.

Dismissing Clara's brother's advice, I relaxed my butt cheeks, scrunched my stomach muscles and silently let a smidgen of gas escape.

I swiftly cleaned up the pencil shavings on the bookcase, making it appear no one was ever there. I dumped the shavings in the wastebasket and snatched my pencil from the sharpener.

I casually walked back to my desk as if nothing had happened and slid into my seat. I leaned back in my desk and silently prayed nobody had to sharpen a pencil.

After finishing question four, I slowly lifted my head and cautiously scanned the room. Everything appeared normal.

So far so good.

I began reading question five. Out of the corner of my eye, I spotted Ms. Joyner jerk upright in her chair and grimace.

Oh, great.

Ms. Joyner had made it clear the first week of school she didn't appreciate a kid passing gas in class. She had warned us if she caught a student stinking up her room, the kid had to write a long essay about farting in English.

My chest tightened, my heart rate increased and the hair on my arms stood on end like blades of grass. Rivers of sweat slithered down my sides, and my fingers trembled.

Is this what a panic attack feels like?

I read question five with my hands tucked in my lap, otherwise my fingers would give me away.

Ms. Joyner leaned forward in her chair and looked out at the class, her nostrils quivering. "Someone cut the cheese. Does anyone want to accept blame for fouling up my room?"

In the silence that followed, I heard my heart pounding in my chest.

Nobody raised a hand.

Ms. Joyner wrinkled her nose so her specs rose up to her eyes. She loudly sniffed the air three times. "Someone broke wind in the back of the room. Does anyone in the back row want to come clean?"

No one fessed up.

She's gonna blame somebody else. Two of us must've farted at the same time.

I didn't believe my luck. I relaxed. My fingers stopped shaking, my breathing returned to normal and my heart rate slowed down.

I twisted around in my desk and checked out the five kids in the back row. Ian blew his nose, Erin stared at the ceiling and Mary bit her nails. Mike peered out the window and Bill coughed into his sleeve.

Ms. Joyner pushed herself from her chair and started pacing back and forth in front of the room. Every so often she paused, tilted her back and sniffed the air like a bird dog hunting pheasant.

"It's not anyone in the back row," Ms. Joyner told the class as she passed my desk for a second time. "But the smell did originate somewhere in the back of the room."

Boy, Clara's brother wasn't kidding.

As the kids in the back row heaved loud sighs of relief, my panic returned.

My muscles tensed and my heart beat wildly. Sweat poured off my forehead. Desperate, I played a toddler version of hide-and-seek. I covered my eyes with my hands, pretending if I couldn't see Ms. Joyner, she couldn't see me.

The teacher inhaled deeply through her nose. "The odor came from the back corner of the room." She sucked in another deep breath. "Near the pencil sharpener."

I don't believe it. She's discovered the location.

"Phil, weren't you sharpening your pencil a minute or so ago?"

So much for hide-and-seek.

When I uncovered my eyes, Ms. Joyner stood over my desk with her hands propped on her hips. Her piercing eyes stared right through me.

I groaned. Busted and with nobody to blame, I confessed. "Yes, Ms. Joyner, I cut the cheese. But can I explain?" I asked before she gave me the third degree.

"It's *may*, not *can*," Ms. Joyner said, correcting my grammar for the gazillionth time. She gave me her you're-hopeless look.

I repeated the question. "May I explain?"

"Can't wait to hear your explanation." Ms. Joyner rolled her eyes toward the ceiling.

I cleared my throat twice.

"I don't have all day, Phil." Her tone left no question she wanted to get back to grading papers.

"Did you know, Ms. Joyner, that a person should break wind at least a dozen times a day for good tummy health?"

"No, I didn't." The teacher sounded annoyed.

"Well, it's a fact."

"I assume you're getting this useful information from the internet?" Ms. Joyner asked in a voice dripping with sarcasm.

"No, a doctor told my father that. At least that's what my father told my mom when he farted at dinner last night. So, you see, I was just following a doctor's advice."

The whole class burst into wild laughter. Even Ms. Joyner cracked a smile, but her good mood lasted only for half a moment. Glaring at the class she said, "Enough," in her firmest teacher's voice.

Ms. Joyner turned her attention to me. "Tomorrow, Phil, you will hand in a 250-word, hand-written essay titled 'Never Pass Wind in English.'"

The teacher removed her glasses, set them on her desk and continued with her mini-lecture. "It must have five paragraphs and follow the rules I laid out in class for writing an essay. If I find more than six mistakes, you'll rewrite it."

A guy in the middle of the room yelled, "Way to go, Stinky Pants."

I stood, turned to my classmates and bowed.

The class laughed good-naturedly.

"Okay, fun's over," Ms. Joyner barked. The room fell silent. "Now, everybody get busy."

I worked on my assignment until the bell rang ending class.

Shane and CJ caught up with me in the hallway. "Nice work, Mr. Tooters," CJ said and smiled.

"Didn't you try any of my hold-a-fart tricks I taught you last year?" Shane asked.

"Yeah, but it's impossible to keep your butt cheeks clenched for over nine minutes," I said, now sandwiched between Shane and CJ in a hallway packed with kids.

"Yeah. That's a long time," Shane said. "My record is six."

I was about to congratulate Shane when CJ jumped into the conversation. "Well, you did it, Phil."

"Whaddaya talking about?"

"Watching Joyner act like a springer spaniel was hilarious," CJ said.

"I'll say," Shane added, "and your comment about your father, priceless."

"I'm glad I amused you guys," I said in jest as the three of us stopped at my locker. "Joyner is clueless. She doesn't know the difference between a fraction and a contraction." CJ and Shane laughed.

McKenzie Harper and two of her friends paraded past us holding their noses. "Shame. Shame. Shame," McKenzie taunted. She tossed her long, straight hair over her shoulder and giggled.

"Hey, Harper. Do you slice carrots with that nose?" I shouted as she strutted down the hallway, her hair bouncing on her shoulders with every stride.

"If you were twice as smart, you'd still be stupid," she shouted back as she and her friends disappeared around the corner.

I flung open my locker and grabbed my science book. "And to think at one time I thought she was cute. I must've been crazy."

"Forget about her," Shane said as I slammed my locker shut.

"Yeah," CJ agreed. "Let's get going before we're late for second hour."

My friends and I set off for science but stopped for a traffic jam in the hallway. "I hate writing essays, especially long ones," I said, while we waited for the crowd to scatter.

"That's why you never fart in English," CJ replied with a grin.

"That's why I always fart in a foreign language," Shane added. My friends cracked up, but I was in no mood to laugh.

After doing my homework that evening, I dug my English book out of my backpack. I opened my textbook and read the chapter titled "Tips for Writing an Essay."

Once done, I hauled out an old notebook from the desk drawer, found a blue pen and began writing. After forty-five minutes of agony, I set my pen on the desk and counted the words: 259.

More than enough.

I proofread my essay three times, looking for grammar, spelling and punctuation mistakes. Satisfied there were none, I got ready for bed and set my alarm ten minutes earlier than usual. I wanted to check over my essay one last time before heading to school.

I crawled into bed, pulled up the covers and turned off the lamp on the nightstand. Before drifting off to sleep, I promised myself I'd never again break wind in English. If I needed to fart, I'd pretend to be sick, dash from the room and pass gas while running down the hallway to the john.

One thing for sure, no more long essays for me.

RULE THREE

NEVER CUT DETENTION

I have my father to thank for my three nights of detention.

Weeks earlier my parents had received an email from Mr. Huxley, my math teacher. The email informed them I had two missing assignments and had flunked a recent quiz. Due to the missing work and the failed quiz, I had a D average.

My parents panicked and put together an action plan to raise my grade. After making sure I handed in my missing work, they began reviewing my math homework and studying for quizzes and tests with me.

My father popped into my room as I was putting my laptop to sleep. "Hey, son. Math done?"

"Didn't know you were a poet, Dad."

"Clever, Phil. Now let's go over math."

I flipped open my math folder, pulled out my assignment and handed it to my father. "I have two worksheets. One is changing fractions to decimals. The other is converting decimals to fractions."

"I'm more concerned with converting your D to a B," Dad said with a grin.

Dad plunked down on the edge of my bed and made himself comfortable. As he looked over the first worksheet, his phone rang. Dad set the worksheets on the bed, pulled his phone from his pocket and checked the screen.

"Hey, Sam, what's up?" I didn't know Sam, but by the expression on my father's face the call was important. "Hold on a minute, Sam."

Dad stood and faced me. "Phil, I have to take this call downstairs. It's work and I need some items from my briefcase."

Dad picked up the worksheets and hustled toward the door. "I'll look over your assignments in my office and return them when I'm done."

"Fine." I grabbed my phone from my desk and checked my messages.

Dad hesitated for a moment in the doorway. "Be

back shortly, son." The door swung closed behind him with a loud thud.

I forgot about the worksheets until the next morning. As the bus rumbled into the school's parking lot, my phone pinged in my pocket. I reached into my jeans and dug out my phone. My father's text message read, "Call me, ASAP."

"Check this out." I showed CJ the text as the bus slowly pulled up to the drop-off area. "Whaddaya think that's about?"

"Beats me," said CJ, who sat next to me scarfing down a snack bag of Cheetos.

I punched in my father's number as the bus driver pushed the handle to open the door. Dad answered after one ring. "Hi, Phil."

"What's up, Dad?" I stood and waited in line.

"I'm at the office and found your worksheets in my briefcase. Must've stuck them there after my phone call last night."

"What?" I said, inching down the aisle toward the door. "You gotta be kidding."

"Wish I were, son. I apologize. I'm tied up all day so I can't run the worksheets to school. If you need an excuse, have your teacher call me. Have to run."

I shut off my phone and hopped off the bus, shaking my head.

"What's up?" CJ asked as we strode into school.

"You look like you've seen a ghost."

I slipped my phone into my back pocket. "My father took my math assignment to work."

"That's NOT good," CJ said, as we threaded our way through the loud hallway to our lockers.

"You got that right."

"Can he bring the worksheets to school?"

"No. He's busy all day," I replied, almost running into a girl scurrying in the opposite direction.

"Huxley isn't gonna be happy," CJ said in a I'm-glad-I'm-not-you tone.

"Tell me something I don't know. Math should be a barrel of laughs."

After lunch, I grabbed my math materials from my locker and headed to fifth hour prepared for the worst. Mr. Huxley stood by his oversized desk as I stepped into the room.

The teacher, who looked to be my father's age, was like usual, well dressed. He wore a short-sleeve dress shirt, pressed pants and fancy tie.

Once Mr. Huxley took roll, he sauntered over to the lectern and stood behind it. "Get out your worksheets so we can correct and grade them."

My hand shot up.

"What is it, Phil?" Mr. Huxley asked, a trace of impatience in his voice.

"My assignment is done, Mr. Huxley, but I don't

have it with me."

The teacher rested his elbows on the metal lectern and stared straight at me. "What's your compelling reason this time, Phil?"

I explained what happened. "If you want to call my father, the number is 920-72—"

Mr. Huxley cut me short with a wave of his hand. "No reason to. No matter who's at fault, you don't have your homework," he said with a cold edge to his voice. "You'll receive two zeros, and I want both worksheets when you walk into my room tomorrow. Understand?"

"Yes, Mr. Huxley."

The teacher strolled over and picked up his record book lying on the corner of his desk. He opened the book, jotted something down and studied the page for a few seconds.

Mr. Huxley closed the book, set it on his desk and looked at me. "Checking my records, Phil, this is your third missed assignment this quarter. For three days, starting tomorrow, you'll report to after-school detention."

I sat bolt upright in my desk. "Seriously?"

"I told you the first day of class you get two freebies per grading period. The third time it's detention, and it's one day for each missed assignment."

"Three days. You gotta be kidding me!"

"Actually, Phil, I'm giving you a break." Mr. Huxley

straightened his bright blue tie. "If I counted each worksheet separately, you would've earned four nights of detention."

"Some break," I mumbled.

The teacher's eyes narrowed as he glared at me. "Did you say something, Phil?"

A half-dozen thoughts flashed through my mind. Knowing I'd get in more trouble, I bit my tongue to stop myself from saying something else stupid. "No, Mr. Huxley."

"Good." He waved an orange detention pad in the air. "Get your slip when you leave."

Forty-five minutes later, I stomped out of class with a detention slip crumpled in my back pocket.

At dinner, I mentioned what had happened in math to my father. He wanted to phone Mr. Huxley, but I told him not to bother. The call would not change the teacher's mind.

√   √   √

The next day after school, I reported to detention or, as my friends and I call it, "Happy Hour." I trudged into Room 123 not knowing what to expect.

Five rows across, six tables deep, divided up the windowless double classroom. Three boys sat at every other table in rows one and five. Three girls were seated at every other table in row three. They all worked quietly.

A glum-faced man with acne-filled cheeks sat behind a messy desk in the front center of the room. His unkempt hair looked like it had been cut with a hedge trimmer. Printed on the desk plate was Mr. Runyon. Under his name was Detention Supervisor.

He quit working on a crossword puzzle in the newspaper, tilted his head to the side and fixed his eyes on me. "You are?"

"Phil Abrams." I handed him my detention slip.

He peered at his attendance sheet, crossed off my name and checked the time. "You're three minutes late, Mister Abrams. Detention starts at 3:15."

"I didn't realize they moved the room. Last year detention was in 206."

We locked eyes. "Since you're such an expert at detention, Abrams, you should know where detention is held."

Mr. Runyon scrunched up my detention slip and tossed it in the trash. "Today, you'll leave three minutes after everyone else," he said in a gruff voice. "If you're late again, you'll be back for an extra night. Got it?"

"Yeah."

The supervisor rambled on. "I'm here because someone has to babysit you numbskulls. These are the rules and I expect them to be followed. You may do homework or read."

Mr. Runyon brushed away what appeared to be dandruff flakes from his shoulder and continued his spiel. "No talking. No questions. No napping. No phone and No exceptions. Leaving the room is forbidden, including visiting the restroom. Dismissal is 4:15. Understand?"

I didn't answer because the zits on his face had diverted my attention. Dozens of pimples peppered his cheeks and nose, and the zit on his chin looked like a huge red Skittle.

"It's not a trick question, Abrams."

When I didn't respond, he snapped his fingers in my face, jolting me from my thoughts.

"Huh?"

"Do you understand the rules, Abrams?" he asked in a surly voice.

I nodded.

"If you find yourself with nothing to do, read a magazine or book." Mr. Runyon pointed to a dusty bookcase piled high with teetering stacks of magazines and paperbacks. "If that doesn't appeal to you, *focus* on why you're in detention," he said, a touch of anger creeping into his voice. "Clear?"

"Yup." I now knew now why students called Room 123 the Focus Room.

Mr. Runyon surveyed the room. "Now sit, there."

He pointed at the second table in the second row.

I sat crosswise from a boy and a girl, neither of whom I knew. For the next fifty-four minutes, I finished my math and social studies homework and studied for a science quiz.

Once done, I mulled over Mr. Runyon's suggestions to read a magazine or to focus on how I landed in detention. I chucked both ideas.

Instead, I counted the zits on Mr. Runyon's face. After losing count for the fourth time, I turned his face into an astronomy lesson. I spent the last minutes of detention connecting zits.

Seven zits on his right cheek resembled the Little Dipper. The jumbo zit on his chin became the North Star, and I named five zits running across his left cheek the Northern Cross.

While I tried locating the Big Dipper, Mr. Runyon announced, "It's 4:15. All of you may leave except Mister Abrams."

After twiddling my thumbs for three minutes, I strolled out of the Focus Room.

When I plodded into detention the second day, the same girl sat diagonally across from me. But Chad Cooper, a seventh grader who reeked of BO, now sat crosswise on my right.

A man among boys, Cooper was so big the top of my head came up to his armpits. A one-man wrecking crew and a big-time troublemaker, he had made the vice-principal's office his second home.

"Okay, lunkheads. It's 3:15." Mr. Runyon opened his newspaper to the crossword puzzle page and set the paper on his desk. "Detention has begun."

I took out my math and science books and worked on my assignments. Besides completing two math worksheets and six science questions, I studied for a vocabulary test. By the time I finished my homework, only seven minutes remained.

I gazed at Cooper, who sat biting the eraser off his pencil. When he flicked a look over his shoulder, Cooper caught me staring at him. "Whaddaya staring at?" he whispered with a sneer.

"Nothing," I whispered back, but I wasn't sure he heard me.

Seconds later, Mr. Runyon checked his phone and stood. "I have to be gone for a short time. If I catch anyone fooling around when I get back, I'll add two nights of detention." The teacher hurried from the room.

Immediately, Cooper got up, scurried over to Mr. Runyon's desk and snatched a stapler.

What was he gonna do with a stapler?

Cooper popped open the stapler and marched over to my table.

Thump.   ThumpThumpThump.   Thump.
ThumpThumpThumpThump.

Everybody cracked up except me. I sat there red-faced, peering at my math worksheets plastered to the table.

"Next time, Abrams, mind your own business." Cooper closed the stapler and put it back on the teacher's desk. As Cooper slid into his chair, Mr. Runyon stepped back into the room.

Hearing snickers, the teacher asked, "What's going on in here?"

Silence filled the room.

The teacher eyed all of us suspiciously. He said nothing, but he didn't look happy.

Using the tip of my pen as a screwdriver, I spent the last minutes of detention prying my worksheets free. As I dug out the ninth staple, Mr. Runyon announced, "Everybody may leave."

I collected my books but waited until everyone had left. I scooped up the staples, tossed them in the wastebasket and scooted out the door.

I strode into detention on my last day and found Cooper slumped in his seat. He sat with his long legs stretched out under the table, cleaning his fingernails with a paper clip.

As I set my binder and math book on the table, a girl standing crosswise from me caught my eye. About my height, her wavy brown hair hung to the sides of her oval face. Freckles sprinkled her cheeks and a pair of rose-colored glasses sat on her slim nose.

She smiled at me and a cute dimple appeared at the corner of her mouth. I smiled back as we slipped into our hard plastic chairs.

I had seen this girl before, but where?

"It's 3:15, knuckleheads," Mr. Runyon announced. "The start of your favorite hour."

I had little homework, so after finishing math, I read outdated magazines. From time to time, my eyes strayed in the direction of the freckle-faced girl. She sat with her feet hooked around the back legs of her chair, lost in a paperback novel.

With three minutes left, I returned the magazines and lumbered back to my seat. Once there, my thoughts shifted to Cooper. He had lots of problems in school, but having too many smarts wasn't one of them. He had been held back in kindergarten and had flunked third grade. I was thirteen, so that made him fifteen.

In eighth grade, Cooper would be sixteen and old enough to drive. I pictured him parking his rusty pickup truck with a jacked-up rear end and a dented front fender in the teachers' parking lot. I grinned as I imagined the looks on the teachers' faces.

"Everyone's free to leave," Mr. Runyon announced.

I grabbed my book and binder, but as I left, I tripped over the leg of my table. As I tried regaining my balance, I collided with the girl who had been sitting crosswise from me. The collision sent her books and pencil case flying.

"I'm sorry." I gave her a sheepish smile.

"No biggie." She straightened her glasses and bent over to scoop up her books.

"Here, let me help." I crouched down and picked up the novel she had been reading, but as I stood, I clunked my head on the table.

The girl clapped her hand over her mouth to stifle a giggle. "You okay?"

"Yeah, fine." I handed the girl her book.

"Thanks. I'm Ellen. Ellen Stratton."

That's it. She's the girl who read announcements.

"Glad to meet you, Ellen. I'm Phil. Phil Abrams."

We walked out of the room together, stopped in the hallway and texted our parents to pick us up.

"Oh, no." Ellen shook her head.

"What's the matter?"

"My father's car has a flat, and he can't get here for half an hour."

"No problem," I said, pocketing my phone. "My mom will be here in about eight minutes. She'll drive you home."

"Really? Are you sure, Phil?"

"Yeah."

"Great. I'll text my dad and tell him he doesn't have to come get me."

As we strolled to our lockers, I learned Ellen got detention for reading a text during class. "I'll meet you by the front entrance," I told her as we split up. I watched her stride down the hallway until she turned the corner.

I dumped my book and binder in my locker, slipped on a jacket and met Ellen at the main entrance.

While we waited in the lobby for our ride, I found Ellen easy to talk to. I discovered she was a good student, enjoyed watching adventure movies and loved playing softball.

Mom drove up to the pick-up area right on time. Ellen and I approached the SUV, and I opened the passenger door. "Mom, this is Ellen. Her dad's car has a flat. Can you drive her home?"

"You bet." Mom looked at Ellen. "Jump in."

Ellen opened the back door and hopped in. I slid into the passenger seat.

Mom glanced over her shoulder and eased away from the curb. "Where do you live, Ellen?"

"On Wilson Street, 1485."

"I know right where that street is. My bridge partner lives a block over."

On the way, I talked Mom into pulling into a fast-food drive-thru. Mom bought each of us a burger, fries and a chocolate shake.

On the way to Ellen's, we devoured our food. We

finished our meals as the SUV crept to a stop in the driveway. Motion sensor lights on the garage and front porch lit up the area.

Ellen opened the door and hopped out. "I have nothing to do tonight, Phil. Do you want to come in and watch movies?"

I sat dumfounded. I tried to say something witty, but it was like I had a gob of peanut butter stuck to the roof of my mouth. My lips parted but no words came out, so I nodded.

"Great," Ellen said.

"Can you pick me up, Mom?" I mumbled, still shaken by Ellen's question.

"Your father will."

"Nice to have met you, Mrs. Abrams. Thanks for the ride and the burger." Ellen closed the door.

Mom rolled down the passenger-side window, unbuckled her seatbelt and leaned past me. "You're welcome, Ellen. A pleasure meeting you."

As Mom rolled up the window, she directed her attention to me. "Your father will come and get you at 10:00."

"It's Friday, Mom. How about 10:30?" I asked, stepping from the SUV.

"Ten." Mom buckled her seatbelt. "And, Phil, remember the rule."

"Yeah, Mom." I peeled off my jacket, tossed it

onto the front seat and closed the door.

"You have a rule about being picked up?" Ellen asked as the SUV backed out of the driveway.

"She means be ready at 10:00 sharp," I said as we strolled side by side up the short walkway. "My parents are sticklers for being on time."

We climbed three steps to the small concrete porch. Ellen fished the house key from her jacket pocket and unlocked the door. She flicked on the lights as we walked inside.

As we stood in the entryway, Ellen said, "We need to take off our shoes, Phil. My mother doesn't want anything scratching her wood floors."

Ellen stripped off her jacket, hung it in the closet and slipped out of her shoes. I kicked off my scuffed-up tennis shoes, thankful I hadn't worn my socks with holes in the toes.

"You can sit over there." Ellen pointed to an overstuffed sofa in the den. "I'll let my mom know I'm home and make us some popcorn."

The cozy room looked like it had never been lived in. I planted myself on one end of a cushy sofa. A short time later Ellen and a tall, slender woman sauntered in. Ellen carried a jumbo bowl of popcorn.

The lady walked over and introduced herself. "I'm Mrs. Stratton, Ellen's mom."

"Nice to meet you, Mrs. Stratton. I'm Phil Abrams."

"Would you like something to drink, Phil?"

"No thanks."

"Well then, I'll leave you two alone." Mrs. Stratton switched on a floor lamp and left the room.

Ellen picked up the remote lying on a footstool and turned on the TV. She plopped down on the sofa, setting the bowl between us. "We can share."

For the next four and a half hours, Ellen and I watched movies, munched popcorn, played video games and finished off a small pepperoni pizza.

I was having so much fun I lost track of time until a horn beeped in the driveway. I glanced at the clock on the mantle above the fireplace: 10:00.

Why couldn't my father be late just this once?

"That's my ride."

Ellen checked her phone. "You weren't kidding about your parents being on time. Mine are usually fifteen minutes late."

We popped up from the sofa and Ellen escorted me into the entryway. "Thanks for coming over, Phil. I had a good time."

"Me too." I slid my feet into my shoes. "Thanks for inviting me and for the popcorn and pizza."

"You're welcome." Ellen opened the door and flashed me a smile that could melt a hockey rink. Speechless, I turned and floated toward the car as Ellen closed the door behind me.

During the ride home, my father talked about the upcoming Packers-Bears game, but I didn't hear a word. Instead, I replayed in my mind one of the most incredible nights of my life.

When I got home, I headed upstairs and plopped down at my desk. I dug out my Rules of Never notebook from the bottom drawer, found a pen and opened the notebook to page three. At the top of the page, I wrote RULE THREE: "NEVER CUT DETENTION."

I closed the notebook and stowed the pen inside the wire loops. I returned the notebook to the drawer, got ready for bed and played video games.

But the whole time I thought about Ellen. She was clearly out of my league. I wasn't talented, athletic or smart. Plus, I was a year behind her in school.

They say things happen for a reason. If my father hadn't taken my homework, I never would've ended up staying after school. No detention, no Ellen. If I get detention again, I'm not going to gripe. Who knows, I might even see Ellen.

An hour later, I hauled myself to bed and crawled under the covers. I switched off the lamp on my nightstand and drifted off to sleep thinking how cool it would be to have Ellen as a girlfriend.

NEVER PLAY AN ELF IN A SCHOOL SKIT

Ever wish you'd never gotten out of bed in the morning?

"Settle down, kids, and listen up," Ms. Joyner said as she strode over to the TV. She switched on the TV, ambled back to her desk and sat down.

"Good morning, fellow Frogs," Principal Knox said. "Today is Wednesday, December 9. The high today will be forty-six. Bring a jacket if you are planning to go outside after lunch."

The principal smoothed out his checkered tie. "A big thank you to Mrs. Quinn, our librarian, for making the

Book Fair a big success. The $188 raised will be used to spruce up the media center."

Principal Knox peeked at his notes lying on the table. "A reminder to all seventh-grade homeroom teachers. If you haven't already, please send the name of your representative for the winter holiday skit to the office by the end of the day."

The principal flipped over his notes. "Now, here's Amelia, your Student Council secretary, to tell you what's happening at Lost Creek."

"Thank you, Principal Knox," Amelia said. "Today's lunch menu is breaded chicken or fish tacos, corn, salad and dried fruit. The wrestling team has a meet at Hillcrest Middle School at 4:30. The Chess Club meeting has been cancelled. That's it for now. Have a fantabulous day."

Ms. Joyner rose from her chair, strolled over and shut off the TV. She picked up a piece of paper lying on a lectern that appeared to be a memo.

The teacher turned and faced the class. "As you heard," she said with little enthusiasm, "one of you has to participate in the holiday skit. Is there a volunteer or must I pick someone?"

"Can you tell us about the skit, Ms. Joyner?" asked Vicki, who used a wheelchair to make her way around school.

"Certainly, Vicki," the teacher said. "It's an annual

skit put on by and for seventh graders before winter break. After the skit, the seventh-grade band and chorus perform."

"When are rehearsals?" CJ asked.

Ms. Joyner checked the memo in her hand. "Next week Tuesday and Thursday. The week after that, rehearsals are Monday and Tuesday, and the skit is Wednesday morning. Now, does anyone want to volunteer?"

No one uttered a peep or raised a hand.

"A skit is a great way to make new friends," Ms. Joyner said. "Any budding actors out there?"

Dead quiet.

Ms. Joyner tried a different approach. "As an incentive, I'll add ten points to the volunteer's next English quiz."

Nobody bit.

She upped her offer. "How's ten points on Friday's exam?"

A thousand points wouldn't be enough.

Ms. Joyner pressed on. "I don't want to choose someone, but I'll be forced to if no one volunteers. Ten points on the next quiz, ten points on Friday's exam and a hundred on tomorrow's spelling test. Final offer."

Still no takers.

"Then I have to select somebody," she said, a note of irritation in her voice.

Ms. Joyner's eyes traveled up and down the rows searching for a possible victim. I turned in my desk and surveyed the room. Students sat stone-still with fearful expressions on their faces. A few appeared to be praying they wouldn't be chosen.

When Ms. Joyner eyed up my row, she zeroed in on me. "Phil, you'd be perfect for the part."

"I can't, Ms. Joyner. I'll be performing with the band and won't have time to change clothes."

"No problem, Phil. The memo mentions nothing about costumes. Besides, if you're in costume, wear it while the band is on stage."

"Oh, I just remembered. I have to babysit my sister after school next week," I said, trying to find a way out of a skit I wanted no part of.

"That's not a problem either, Phil. Rehearsal starts at 7:00 PM."

Out of excuses, I slumped across my desk and groaned.

"Okay, class, now that's settled, let's move on to today's lesson." While the teacher set the memo on her desk, Shane raised his hand. "Yes, Shane."

"One question, Ms. Joyner."

"Make it quick, Shane." The teacher adjusted her silver necklace.

"Does Phil get the bonus points on the quiz and exam and a hundred on the spelling test?"

Never thought of that. At least I'll get something out of this.

Ms. Joyner shifted her eyes to me. "No, because he didn't volunteer."

Why am I not surprised?

"Now, class, log on to your laptop and bring up your descriptive paragraph so we can go over it."

√   √   √

On Tuesday, I arrived at skit practice early and sat on stage chatting with the other performers. A short, plump woman wearing a pea-green dress was talking to a man who struck me as a stage hand.

When the woman spun around, I recognized her. She was Mrs. Fox, the head of Lost Creek's gifted and talented program.

Mrs. Fox called us over. "Please line up." Within seconds, nine girls and three boys stood in a row facing Mrs. Fox.

"Welcome everybody. I'm Mrs. Fox, Lost Creek's Gifted and Talented Coordinator. I'll be directing this year's skit. Now, please introduce yourself."

After hearing our names, Mrs. Fox asked, "How many of you have ever performed on stage?"

No one raised a hand.

"How many of you are nervous?"

Everybody put up a hand except me.

I raised both hands high in the air.

"Three thoughts to ease everyone's mind," Mrs. Fox said. "First, the skit has just three speaking parts, Santa and two reindeer. Second, there's one song, "Jingle Bells," but we sing the carol together. Third, the skit is only thirteen minutes long."

Thirteen minutes can be an eternity. Ask anyone in Joyner's English class.

"Now, here's your role." The director studied a three by five card she held in her hand.

I silently recited a short prayer I wouldn't have a speaking part.

"Victoria will play Santa, and Lana and Addison will be reindeer. The rest of you will play elves."

I gave a nod of thanks to the heavens.

We spent the rest of the time practicing. The three main actors took center stage and read through their parts. Within minutes I knew why Mrs. Fox chose Victoria to play Santa. Cheerful, poised and charming, she was perfect for the lead role.

Nine elves stood in the background holding large props such as an ornament, a snowflake and a wrapped present. My prop was a sack of toys.

At the end of the skit, the twelve of us sang "Jingle Bells." Mrs. Fox quickly discovered that even though six girls and Mason took chorus, most of them were space fillers. And Lucas and I couldn't carry a tune in a bucket.

Except for singing "Jingle Bells," practice went fine. I left rehearsal thinking if I lip-synced the song, being on stage might be okay.

After all, I just stood there holding a prop.

At Thursday's practice, my enthusiasm playing an elf fizzled out like a damp firecracker. As the twelve of us stood waiting around for rehearsal to begin, Mrs. Fox announced, "Please join me in the middle of the stage."

We walked over and surrounded Mrs. Fox. "I've tweaked a few parts in the skit." The director reeled off some minor adjustments, like the time the elves appeared on stage and where the reindeer were to stand.

Mrs. Fox checked the clipboard she was holding. "I also made two major changes. Victoria, Lana and Addison will sing "Jingle Bells" at the end of the skit while the elves sway to the music."

I breathed a sigh of relief and gave Lucas, who stood beside me, a hearty thumbs-up.

Mrs. Fox then dropped a bombshell that gave me the willies. "Phil, I expanded your role. At the end of the skit you will walk up to Santa, say a few words and hand him the sack of toys."

I gulped. "What?" I asked, my heart in my throat. "You told us elves didn't have to say anything."

"I know, but the ending flows much better with this slight revision."

"Why can't some other elf do it?"

"Because you're the elf holding the sack of toys. Besides, it's just one short line." Mrs. Fox gently placed her hand on my shoulder. "All you have to say is, 'Santa, here's the toys for the boys and girls' and hand Santa the sack."

Before I protested again, Mrs. Fox announced, "Okay, kids, let's practice these changes."

Toward the end of the skit and with my heart hammering like crazy, I marched up to the sleigh and nervously recited my line. "Santa, here's the boys for the toys and girls." The other eleven actors burst out laughing.

After everyone had quieted down, Mrs. Fox said, "Phil, your line is, 'Santa, here's the toys for the boys and girls.'"

"I know, but I freaked out."

"You can do this, Phil. Now, let's practice the skit once more before we end for the week."

By the time it came to my speaking part, I had repeated my line a hundred times in my head. I had my line down pat. But when I walked up to Santa, I bumped into the cardboard sleigh, knocking it over.

Mrs. Fox let out an exasperated sigh. "Let's wrap it up for the night. I'll see everybody Monday."

I left practice bummed.

While sitting next to CJ on the school bus during our ride home on Monday, I received a text message from Mrs. Fox. "Report to the dressing room behind the stage before practice."

"Why would Mrs. Fox want to meet in the dressing room?" I asked CJ.

"Duh. To try on costumes."

"Costumes? No one said anything about costumes."

"Then it's probably nothing."

Probably nothing turned into definitely something.

Though I arrived for practice early, the other actors were already in the dressing room. They sat in small groups talking among themselves. I took a seat alongside Mason.

"Now that we are all here, I have some marvelous news," Mrs. Fox said. "They delivered our costumes Friday, so before rehearsal we are trying them on."

My jaw dropped to the floor.

"The costumes are delightful," she said.

I bet.

The director pulled a costume off a hanger, held up the outfit and gushed, "Aren't these the cutest?"

Define cute.

"No costume will fit perfectly." Mrs. Fox pointed to a tall, casually dressed woman. "This is Mrs. Maxwell, the high school Family and Consumer Ed teacher. If your costume needs alterations, she'll make your outfit look amazing."

"Where do we change, Mrs. Fox?" Victoria asked eagerly.

"Girls dress here. Boys will change in the art room." Mrs. Fox checked her watch. "See you on stage at 7:35 wearing your costumes."

When Lucas, Mason and I moseyed into the art room, Mr. Dixon, a seventh-grade math teacher, greeted us. "Hi, guys. I have five costumes: three medium, one large and one small. Sizing up the three of you, I'd say you all wear medium."

He handed each of us a costume. "Try these on. If something doesn't fit, we'll make adjustments by using the extra costumes."

Twenty minutes later, I stood on stage wearing a cone-shaped red hat and a green jacket that almost reached my knees. Red and white striped tights and red boots with curled-up toes rounded out my outfit.

"Everyone looks adorable," Mrs. Fox said.

Being adorable in front of hundreds of classmates was not on my bucket list.

Mrs. Fox rattled on. "Mrs. Maxwell won't have to make any major alterations. Minor adjustments will be made during rehearsal today and tomorrow. We'll practice the skit twice and quit for the night."

After rehearsal, Mrs. Fox held up a wooden hanger. "You will find a hanger with your name on it in your dressing room. Hang your jacket and tights on the hanger and give the hanger, boots and hat to Mrs. Maxwell or Mr. Dixon. After handing in your costume, you may leave."

"Is tomorrow a full-dress rehearsal, Mrs. Fox?" Addison asked.

"Yes. Everyone be on stage by 7:15 with your costume on. Have a great evening."

"You've gotta be kidding me with these costumes. My legs look like giant lumpy candy canes," I said to Mason and Lucas as we strode down the deserted hallway. "When our friends see us in tights, they'll tease us for the rest of our lives."

"I'll say, but it's too late to do anything about it now," Lucas said.

"It's never too late, Lucas," I said, stopping to pull up my tights, now bunched around my ankles. "A guy could get hurt, lose his voice or catch the flu."

"I'm praying for a huge snowstorm," Mason added.

"Fat chance of that happening," Lucas said.

About halfway to our dressing room, Mason made a ninety-degree turn.

"Where ya going? The art room is this way." I pointed to the opened door at the far end of the long, dimly lit hallway.

"I know, but I gotta pee. Be back in a minute. Wait for me." Mason headed into the restroom.

Not wanting to be seen in our costumes, Lucas and I stood impatiently in the doorway of the Tech Ed room. After some time, Mason reappeared. "What took you?" Lucas asked. "We almost called the cops."

"Funny, Lucas," Mason said. "But have either of you ever taken a whiz in an elf's costume?"

"Nope," I said while Lucas shook his head.

"Well, neither have I. It's a hassle. You hafta lift up your jacket, pull down your tights, hold up the jacket and then go."

"Duh. Why didn't you take your jacket off first?" Lucas asked.

Mason slapped his forehead with his palm. "Wish I would've thought of that." Lucas and I laughed as the three of us strolled into the art room to change clothes.

After changing, Mason and Lucas took off to catch their rides. I headed to my locker to retrieve my laptop. On the way, I texted Mom to pick me up.

The next day at rehearsal everything fell into place. No one flubbed a line or stumbled on stage. The twelve actors gathered around Mrs. Fox before leaving. "If you perform tomorrow like you did tonight, you'll be a huge hit," the director said. "I'm so excited."

I'm glad somebody is.

"I'll see all of you in the morning at 10:15," Mrs. Fox said. "You may leave."

As I left the stage, I texted Mom to come get me. I changed, handed the outfit to Mr. Dixon and took off. By the time I reached the front entrance, Mom was waiting for me.

On my ride home I checked the weather app on my phone, hoping Mason's prayers would be answered. Not even a chance of flurries was in the forecast. The skit was on.

Exhausted from running a million laps in PE, I went to bed early, but tossed and turned much of the night. I spent half the night worrying about messing up my line.

The other half I thought about the razzing I'd endure after classmates saw my costume. Before falling asleep, I vowed never again to wear an elf's outfit.

The next morning I rolled over in bed and eyed my alarm clock. The large red numbers glared 9:30. I tore off the covers, jumped out of bed and yelled downstairs. "Mom, why didn't you wake me up?"

"For what?" She yelled back.

"School."

"Called off, so I turned off your alarm."

I slipped on some sweatpants, sprinted down the stairs and flew into the kitchen. "School's called off? What happened?"

"A water pipe burst and flooded the cafeteria."

"Whoopee!"

"I figured you'd be happy, but what about the skit you've been working on?"

"It's a shame I can't take part," I fibbed.

"Well, get dressed and I'll make you chocolate chip pancakes."

As I showered, I thought about the play. Tomorrow was the last day before winter break. The boys' and girls' eighth-grade basketball teams took on the teachers in the afternoon in front of the entire school.

Would the school reschedule the skit in the morning?

I threw on some clothes, grabbed my phone and hurried down the stairs into the kitchen. "Mom, aren't you supposed to be at work?"

"Took a vacation day to watch you perform and do some last minute Christmas shopping."

On top of everything else, Mom was coming?

As I plopped into a chair, my phone pinged. I tapped on Mrs. Fox's message.

"SKIT CANCELLED" popped up.

Two of the most beautiful words I've ever read.

RULE FIVE

NEVER UNDERESTIMATE THE POWER OF A GOOD DEED

After Mr. Pittman, my science teacher, Mrs. Ward was my favorite seventh-grade teacher.

Mrs. Ward taught social studies. Fair, patient and funny, the veteran teacher cared about her students. Students liked her and enjoyed taking her class.

Mrs. Ward usually began social studies with a joke. Although the jokes were corny, my friends and I looked forward to them.

"Quiet please," Mrs. Ward said, standing in front of the class.

Students settled down.

The teacher continued. "My eight-year-old granddaughter told me a cute joke last night. What did the Pacific Ocean say to the Atlantic Ocean?"

No one raised a hand.

Mrs. Ward scanned the room. "Anybody?"

Everyone sat baffled. "We give up," Shane cried out.

"Nothing. It just waved."

The whole class groaned.

"Okay. I've wasted enough time." Mrs. Ward ambled over and stood in front of her desk. She reached behind her, picked up a textbook and quickly leafed through it until she found the page she wanted. "Turn to page 107 in your book."

After the class read the chapter on world poverty, Mrs. Ward closed her book and set it on her desk. "As you see, poverty affects over a billion people. Millions of poor people live in the United States. Poverty impacts thousands of citizens in our state and hundreds in our community."

Mrs. Ward leaned back against her desk. "To help needy families in our area during the holidays, I'm attempting something I have never done before. I'm starting a canned food drive."

Shane cut in. "Winter break is a little over three weeks away. Is that enough time, Mrs. Ward?"

"I'm only doing this with my social studies classes, Shane, so it should be."

Mrs. Ward strolled to the front center of the room. "Here's the deal, class. For every three cans of food you bring in, I'll give you one point on any assignment. For example, nine cans gets you three points, twelve cans four points and so on."

"Phil will hafta bring in 200 cans just to pass," CJ shouted.

"Make that 400," I said, triggering an outburst of laughter.

Mrs. Ward stopped chuckling. "Okay, class, let's get back on task."

The room quieted down.

"As I was about to point out," Mrs. Ward said, "most of you have a few cans at home you could donate."

"I'll say," CJ chimed in. "Can't wait to get rid of those green beans my mother buys."

"We have half a dozen cans of beets in our pantry I'll gladly contribute," Clara added.

"Before going hog wild, class, I need to make a few points," Mrs. Ward said. "First, make sure you get your parents' permission before taking food from home. Second, check the can's expiration date. If the date has passed, leave the can home."

Mrs. Ward paused and fiddled with her earring that resembled a fishing lure. "Third, ask your parents to buy an extra can or two to donate the next time they get groceries."

"How many cans do you hope to collect, Mrs. Ward?" Clara asked.

"No idea, Clara. If each of you brings in three cans, this room would donate seventy-five cans. I'm doing this with my three other classes, so that's 300 cans."

"What are you going to do with 300 cans of green beans, Mrs. Ward?" CJ asked.

The teacher chuckled. "Just because you don't like green beans, CJ, doesn't mean every student feels the same way. I'm sure there will be a variety of food."

Mrs. Ward walked over and stood beside her desk. "To answer your question, CJ, the cans will be given to food banks in the area."

The teacher checked the time. "Enough about the food drive. For the remainder of class, work on the chapter review questions on page 116 in your textbook. Due tomorrow."

As I finished question six, the bell rang. "We'll continue our discussion on poverty tomorrow. Have a great rest of your day," Mrs. Ward said as students exited the room.

Since I no longer had computer science, I reported to study hall. I finished social studies, studied for a science test and spent the rest of the period thinking about the food drive. Mrs. Ward had come up with a nice way to help people in need, but 300 cans helped only a few families.

What if the entire school got involved?

I'll spring my brainchild on my friends at lunch to see what they think.

At lunch, I told Shane, CJ and Clara my idea of a schoolwide food drive. All three were supportive.

"How many kids go to Lost Creek?" Shane asked. He leaned over his tray and took a chomp out of his sloppy joe, dripping sauce down his chin.

"Use this." Clara handed Shane her napkin. "Before you ruin your shirt."

"If you two are done fooling around, I'll answer Shane's question." CJ whipped out a phone from his back pocket and opened a calculator app. "Lost Creek has three grades. Each grade has twelve homerooms, so the school has thirty-six homerooms. A homeroom has, let's say, twenty-five students."

CJ punched in twenty-five times thirty-six. "Nine-hundred students. Holy cow!"

"What?" I asked.

"If each student brought in five cans, the school would collect 4500 cans." CJ shoved his phone back into his pocket.

"That's a ton of food," Shane said, dipping a handful of french fries into a mound of ketchup and cramming them into his mouth.

"That would be awesome." I washed down my last bite of roast beef sandwich with chocolate milk. "If I need help with the food drive, will you guys lend a hand?"

CJ gave me a thumbs up.

"For sure," Clara said.

Shane, with his cheeks stuffed, bobbed his head enthusiastically.

"Tomorrow, I'll tell Mrs. Ward our idea and see what she says." I tore open the Snickers wrapper and bit off a chunk of my tasty dessert.

The following day I arrived at social studies early and pitched my food drive proposal to Mrs. Ward.

"That's a wonderful suggestion, Phil, but a schoolwide food drive requires lots of work, and we don't have a lot of time. Can you get some friends to help?"

"I've already talked to them. They're in."

"Then let's brainstorm your idea in class today."

After taking roll, Mrs. Ward pushed her chair away from her desk and stood. "I'm changing course this morning, class. Phil has a project worth pursuing. After he summarizes it, you can share your thoughts on a course of action. Okay, Phil, go ahead."

I stood and began my spiel, but Mrs. Ward cut in. "Phil, speak to the class from the front of the room." I shuffled to the front and nervously explained my schoolwide food drive idea. I ended my brief speech with, "Our slogan would be, 'Yes, WE Can.'"

"That's a catchy slogan, Phil," Mrs. Ward said as I returned to my desk. "Do you have a goal in mind?"

"Not really. Just try to get as many cans as possible."

"Now, class, any ideas how Phil can make the food drive a success?" Mrs. Ward asked, as I made my way back to my desk.

"Phil or someone could speak to every social studies class," Tara suggested.

I flipped open my social studies notebook to make some notes on the inside cover.

"Reminders during morning announcements," Ian called out from the back row.

"Yeah, but have a student say it, not the principal. Means more coming from a peer," John said.

"And the student must be an eighth grader," David pointed out. "Eighth graders don't take too kindly to suggestions from sixth or seventh graders."

"And popular," Jenna added.

"All great points," Mrs. Ward said.

"Have a competition in each grade for the most cans," Bill spouted out. "The homeroom winner gets a prize."

"The winner gets free pizza for lunch," Zoey shouted. "My uncle owns a pizzeria downtown. I'm sure he'd be happy to donate some pizzas to the school."

Zoey just became my new best friend.

"I love your enthusiasm," Mrs. Ward said. "But before we go any further, Phil needs to speak to the teachers and get their approval. Then we'll work out the details and implement your suggestions."

"Maybe you should speak to them, Mrs. Ward. I get

nervous in front of groups, especially teachers."

"Like John mentioned earlier, Phil, the speech would mean more coming from you," Mrs. Ward said. "Besides, if your proposal is approved, you'll speak in front of lots of classes."

Mrs. Ward eyed the calendar pinned to the bulletin board. "Can you make the faculty meeting tomorrow at 3:30 in the library, Phil? This still gives you three weeks for the food drive."

"I guess so," I said with a shrug.

"Great. And class, don't wait to bring in cans of food. Even if Phil doesn't get the okay, we would still have our own food drive. Kids have already brought in some items."

Mrs. Ward pointed to a small pile of cans on the floor below the set of wall maps. "Okay, get out your assignment and textbook. We have to get some work done today."

The following afternoon, Mrs. Ward introduced me to the Lost Creek's faculty. My gut churned and sweat oozed out of every pore as I shuffled across the carpet to the front of the library.

"Okay, Phil, you're on,"

said Mrs. Ward, now facing me. "Relax, you'll do fine."

I cleared my throat and shoved my hands into the front pockets of my hoodie to stop them from shaking. I gathered my thoughts and began. I spoke only briefly, but by the time I had finished, my boxers were drenched in sweat and my shirt clung to my back.

During dinner that evening, Mrs. Ward called and told me the teachers backed my project under two conditions. First, the food drive must end two days before winter break to allow time to box up the cans and distribute them to local food banks.

Second, someone from our class will have to speak to the school's social studies classes. Since talking to thirty-five classes by myself was impossible, Mrs. Ward told me my friends and I would share the load. She'd schedule the speakers and the times.

I thanked Mrs. Ward and texted Shane, Clara and CJ and informed them the food drive was a go. They immediately texted back agreeing to help.

That night, I lay in bed thinking how to get the eighth graders involved. I needed to find an eighth grader who would not only agree to speak to them, but one they'd listen to.

I sat straight up. Ellen Stratton would be perfect. She was popular, well-spoken and Student Council vice president. Eighth grade ate lunch at 12:10. I'd get a hall pass and talk to Ellen tomorrow.

The next afternoon, I slipped out of math and headed to the cafeteria. Once there, I spied Ellen sitting at the far end of a long table in the middle of the crowded lunchroom. Jocks, cheerleaders and Student Council members filled her table.

"You can do this," I muttered to myself, summoning the courage to talk to her. Weaving my way through a maze of tables, I sidestepped eighth graders balancing trays heaped with food. Dozens of eyeballs peered at me as I approached Ellen's table. "Hi, Ellen."

Kids at her table turned and looked at me like I was from outer space.

"What are you doing here, dweeb?" asked the center on the basketball team.

Before I could respond, Ellen said, "Leave him alone, Ryan. He's a friend of mine."

"Sorry, didn't know," Ryan said.

Ellen turned her attention to me. "Don't mind him, Phil, but why are you here?"

"I hafta talk to you for a sec." I rubbed the back of my neck.

"Sure." Ellen motioned for me to sit down. Her friend slid one seat over so I could sit across from Ellen. "What's up, Phil?"

"My social studies class wants to get the entire school involved in a food drive. I'm sort of in charge and I could use your help."

Ellen picked up her beef taco. "Sorry, Phil, but I must eat while we talk." She checked her phone. "Have a meeting in nine minutes." Ellen took a bite, chewed and swallowed. "How can I help?"

"I'd like you to talk to the eighth-grade social studies classes to convince them to take part."

"Are the eighth-grade teachers okay with this?" Ellen took another bite of her taco.

"Yup."

Ellen sipped her milk. "Why me?"

"You're well-liked, popular and kids listen to you. Look who you're sitting with."

Ellen blushed. "Can I have a friend help me? I won't have time to speak to every eighth-grade class."

"Sure."

"Then count me in." Ellen polished off her taco.

"Great." I dug my phone out of my pocket. "What's your friend's name?"

"Ava Butler."

"Who's your and Ava's homeroom teacher? My social studies teacher will want to get in touch with her to schedule your speaking times."

Ellen washed down the taco with a mouthful of milk. "We both have Mrs. Ott."

I put Ava and Mrs. Ott in my contacts and rose to leave. "Thanks a million, Ellen."

"No problem, Phil." Ellen gave me her movie-star

smile and continued eating her lunch.

I left the cafeteria fired up, wishing I was a popular eighth grader. Then maybe I would stand a chance with Ellen.

With the teachers, Ellen, Ava, Zoey's uncle and my friends on board, the project began in earnest.

With Mrs. Ward's help, CJ, Shane, Clara and I took turns leaving social studies to speak to the sixth and seventh graders. Ellen and Ava addressed the eighth graders, while Mrs. Ward and Mrs. Ott spoke to their social studies classes.

Every day an eighth-grade Student Council member promoted the food drive during announcements.

The food drive ended on Tuesday, two days before winter break. I anxiously listened to the Wednesday and Thursday announcements, but the results weren't included. I assumed Principal Knox was waiting until after the holidays to announce the homeroom winners.

The eighth-grade girls' and boys' basketball teams played the teachers Thursday afternoon, so I had shortened classes in the morning. After lunch, I, like the other 900 students, rooted wildly for the eighth-grade teams to beat the teachers.

Neither team won, but both games were fun to watch and time flew by. At the end of the second game, Principal Knox strolled to the middle of the basketball court with a microphone in his hand. "All right, students, quiet down."

The gym fell silent.

"Before you leave for the winter holidays, I'd like to announce the results of the food drive. Please hold your applause till the end. The homeroom pizza party winners are: Mrs. Abbott in sixth grade, Mrs. Ward in seventh and Mrs. Ott in eighth.

Everybody clapped, whistled and hollered.

"Quiet," the principal said.

The noise died down.

"Before announcing the total cans collected, I want to recognize five students for their help with the food drive: Clara Pearson, Shane Olson, Caden Jacobs, Ava Butler and Ellen Stratton."

After everyone applauded, the principal pressed on. "A special thanks goes to Phil Abrams, who came up with the idea of a schoolwide food drive and helped get everybody on board. Please stand, Phil."

Embarrassed by the attention, I reluctantly stood while the students and staff gave me a round of applause.

Following the ovation, the principal said, "Let this be a lesson to every student. Never underestimate the power of a good deed. Many families will have a better holiday because of what you've accomplished."

The principal paused. "Now for the final tally. The total cans collected is 4367. Awesome job, students. Have a great holiday. You're dismissed."

Cheers and whoops erupted throughout the gym.

"Great job, Phil," said CJ, who sat beside me in the bleachers.

"I'll second that," Clara said.

"Me too," Shane added as the four of us made our way down to the court.

"Thanks, but it took a team effort and you guys helped a lot."

"Yeah, but it was your idea," CJ said.

As I made my way from the gym to my locker, a number of students congratulated me.

Several minutes later, while putting on my jacket, someone tapped me on the shoulder. I turned and almost fainted. There stood Ellen. My heart melted.

"Stupendous job, Phil."

"Thanks, but you and Ava deserve credit too."

"We didn't do much. Have to run or I'll miss my bus. Have a great holiday." Ellen flashed me her magnetic smile and, just like that, she disappeared.

I walked out of school with a puffed out chest.

Before falling asleep that evening, I reflected on the food drive's success. Not only did the food drive make the holidays more enjoyable for many families, but I helped myself. After talking to all those classes, my fear of speaking in front of groups had vanished.

NEVER WEAR THE WRONG SIZE SHOES

"Be prepared." The motto was bolted to Principal Knox's office door, right below his nameplate.

The principal made a point of being ready for anything. And when it came to student safety, he followed the motto faithfully, as if it were the school's rallying cry.

Students and staff practiced a variety of emergency drills such as lockdown drills, shelter-in-place exercises and evacuation drills.

Believing "practice makes perfect," Principal Knox made us repeat each drill until we could do it in our sleep. It seemed Lost Creek carried out a safety drill every other week.

We practiced fire drills the most. They started in September and ended in May, with seven in between.

Fire drills provided a welcome break from the school's daily routine. They ate up five to seven minutes of class time and allowed students to stretch their legs. I loved fire drills, especially when they occurred first hour. The more English I missed, the better.

A fire drill in January taught me a valuable lesson.

I was having a terrific day. All my morning classes had gone well for the first time in a week. I had aced a social studies quiz, gotten a B on my spelling test and finished my science homework in study hall.

The only disappointing part of my day was my tennis shoes, which my aunt had given me as a Christmas present. I must've had a growth spurt because when I put them on, they were a tad small.

Since I loved the shoes, I decided they might work if I broke them in, so I wore the shoes to school. Huge mistake. By the time I finished lunch, both of my heels sported painful nickel-sized blisters.

When I hobbled into fifth-hour math, an elderly woman wearing a sweater, slacks and boots stood at Mr. Huxley's desk, reading some papers. I've had a number of substitutes at Lost Creek, but I had never seen this woman before.

She looked weathered, like an old cemetery headstone. Wrinkles covered her square face, and her smoky-gray hair was tied in a bun. The thick-lensed glasses perched on her nose magnified her eyes.

The bell sounded signaling the start of class. "Please take your seats," the substitute said as she plopped down in her chair.

"Gonna be a real drag," I muttered to Zoey as I slid into my desk. "Might get a ton of busy work."

"'Fraid so," Zoey replied. "Remember a month ago when we had a sub. I fell asleep and smacked my head on the edge of my desk. The bump didn't go away for a week."

I smiled, picturing Zoey cruising down the hallway with a "goose egg" in the middle of her forehead.

Once we all settled down and roll was taken, the sub stood, picked up a dry-erase marker from her desk and walked over to the whiteboard. After writing "Mrs. Butler," she turned and faced us.

"Good afternoon, everyone," she said in a warm, pleasant way. "Mr. Huxley went home ill. I'm Mrs. Butler. This is the first time I've subbed at Lost Creek, so I hope you make my time here enjoyable."

My eyelids drooped.

The sub set the marker on the whiteboard tray. "The notes Mr. Huxley left mentioned your class was to play math bingo."

My head jerked up and my eyes popped open.

I loved math bingo.

Playing bingo was a great way to spend fifth hour. Besides the possibility of winning a candy bar, class time flew by.

The game was simple. The teacher either read or jotted down a math problem on the board. Students arrived at a solution, found the answer on the bingo card and put an X in the square. The first player who marked five squares in a row yelled, "Bingo."

Mrs. Butler strolled over and gently set an opened cardboard box on my desk. She handed me five laminated cards, five dry erase markers and five small cloths. I passed four sets back.

As she went from row to row handing out materials, I settled into my seat. I kicked off my shoes to stop them from rubbing against my heels.

After passing out the game pieces, Mrs. Butler placed the box on a table, grabbed a stack of notecards and faced the class. "After I read or write down the question, you have thirty seconds to solve the problem and find the answer on your card. Scratch paper is permitted, but no calculators."

The sub scanned the room. "Everybody ready? Question one," she said, reading from the top notecard in her hand. "Nora uses one and a half cups of butter to make one tray of brownies. How many cups of butter does she need to make eight trays?"

The substitute pressed a button on the stopwatch hanging around her neck. "Begin."

As Mrs. Butler reread the question, I did a quick mental calculation. I scanned my bingo card for the number twelve. I marked X in the square next to the free space in the middle of the card.

"Time's up." Mrs. Butler clicked off the stopwatch, went over to the whiteboard and erased her name. "Question two." The sub snatched a marker from the tray, removed the cap and wrote $6(6/15 + 4/15)$ on the board. "Solve the problem."

I quickly came up with four. I found the answer to the right of the square I had just marked, making three squares in a row.

After question thirteen, my odds of winning the game had greatly improved. I was crossing out my fourth square in a row when Maria shrieked, "Bingo!"

A collective groan rose from the room.

"What is your name, young lady?" Mrs. Butler asked.
"Maria."

"Please come up, Maria, and claim your prize."

Maria rose from her desk and strolled past me. She was, as usual, dressed in the latest style. Everything was in-place, right down to the freckles dotting her face. Maria walked over to the substitute.

"According to Mr. Huxley's instructions, I give this to the winner." The sub handed Maria a slip of paper. "When you turn it in, he will give you your prize."

"Thanks, Mrs. Butler."

"You're welcome, Maria."

As Maria sauntered back to her desk, Mrs. Butler said, "Okay, class, erase the answers from your card. Get ready for the next game."

After surveying the room, Mrs. Butler said, "Here's the first question. Triangle ABC is congruent to triangle DEF. If the measure of angle B is thirty-five degrees, what is the measure of angle E?"

Piece of cake.

As I hunted for a square with a thirty-five, the sub repeated the question. Suddenly, a steady ear-piercing, high-pitched sound filled the four corners of the room.

Fire alarm!

I checked the time. I twisted around in my desk and looked at Zoey, who had her hands clamped over her ears. "This is no drill."

"What do you mean?"

"Look at the time."

Zoey glanced at the clock on the front wall. "Yeah, it's 12:28. So what?"

"The eighth graders are eating lunch."

"You're right! We never have drills during lunch hour." The color drained from Zoey's face.

As the alarm blared, students rose from their desks. "Please remain seated," Mrs. Butler shouted. Everyone sat back down.

The sub hurried to her desk, picked up a green folder and opened it. Her eyes skimmed the information inside. "Leave everything and line up single file along the wall." She pointed to the wall near my desk.

Students calmly and silently left their desks by rows and lined up along the side and back walls. Since I sat in the first seat in the first row, I stood and took my place at the front of the line.

As students lined up, Mrs. Butler scurried over and stood beside me. Reading from a sheet of paper inside the folder, she hollered, "Stay in line. Proceed in an orderly manner. No talking. The last student to leave the room, turn off the lights and close the door."

The substitute closed the folder and yelled, "Class, follow me."

I took two steps and realized in the excitement, I hadn't put on my shoes.

"I'm not leaving without my shoes. It's freezing outside," I told Zoey, who stood right behind me. I turned to go back to my desk, but Mrs. Butler gripped my wrist. "Young man, stay in line."

"Gotta get my shoes."

The sub glanced at my feet. "I'm sorry, but there's no time and I need your help. What's your name?"

"Phil Abrams."

"Okay, Phil. Lead the way."

With the alarm's deafening sound echoing off the walls and metal lockers, I stepped into the hallway. I hustled down the corridor in my stocking feet as fast as possible without running, the sub and classmates right on my heels.

"How far, Phil?" the sub bellowed as we made our way along the escape route marked with flashing red strobe lights.

"Not far. End of the hall, down the stairs, through the doors and into the park."

Within seconds, Zoey and I pushed open the double doors leading to a playground. The sub put up her hand and motioned the line to stop. "Where does the class meet in the park, Phil?"

"Over there." I pointed toward the swing set. "Zoey and I will hold the doors open."

The sub nodded.

"Let's go, class," the sub barked and quickly ushered everyone from the building.

I stood on an ice-cold concrete slab and kept the door open as my classmates hurried outside. I leaned against the door and hopped from one foot to the other to keep my toes from becoming numb.

"Great looking shoes," Shane belted out as he strode past me.

"Thanks. Bought them last night," I yelled back. "They're toasty warm."

When the last student filed out, Zoey and I closed the doors and joined our classmates.

Once we were near the playground equipment, Mrs. Butler stood off to the side, letting the line pass. "Keep moving until you reach the swings."

Twenty-five students quietly waded through the snow-covered playground to the swings. Once there we stopped, turned and faced the school. We stood in line shivering, watching our breath hang in the air.

"I'm freezing," I whispered to Zoey.

"I can't believe you're out here in your stocking feet," Zoey said, rubbing her hands together. "Try jumping up and down to stay warm."

After slipping on my first attempt and stubbing my big toe, I walked in place instead. While I tried to keep warm, the sub opened her folder and found the class roster. A brisk north wind whistled through the leafless trees as she called off our names. Everyone was accounted for.

The fire trucks soon arrived with sirens blaring and lights flashing. Minutes later, an all-clear signal sounded, allowing us to head back inside the building.

By this time my nose hairs had frozen together, my teeth were chattering and my toes didn't move. My classmates and I tromped through the blowing snow and into school.

When I returned to the room, I eased into my desk, peeled off my soaked socks and checked out my feet. Both looked like large strawberry freezer pops.

As I dried off my feet with a tissue, the loudspeaker on the front wall crackled to life. "Excuse the interruption," Principal Knox said. "I want to apologize for the fire  drill. One of the staff accidentally set off the alarm. I hope the drill didn't inconvenience anyone."

"I wasn't bothered in the least," I told Zoey, "but my feet sure were."

"How are your toes?" Zoey asked.

"They hurt. Can't even wiggle them."

During the last minutes of math, while the class played bingo, I massaged my feet.

When the bell rang, I hobbled barefoot into the hallway and shuffled to my locker. I dumped off my soggy socks and my math materials and grabbed my Spanish book.

As I carried my Spanish book in one hand and my shoes in the other, Shane and CJ caught up with me in the congested hallway.

"I guess walking barefoot to class is the latest style," CJ said to Shane.

"Real funny, CJ, but I'm thawing out my toes."

"What were you doing in the park in your stocking feet anyway?" CJ asked.

"I took off my shoes because they were causing blisters on the backs of my heels. I forgot about my shoes until we were leaving the room. The sub wouldn't let me go back and get them."

"I assume frozen toes don't smell, Phil," Shane said.

"Why would you say that?" I asked, sidestepping four giggling cheerleaders.

"Cuz the hallway doesn't stink." Shane and CJ chuckled.

I had no comeback to Shane's bad joke. My feet hurt too much, especially my big toe. I limped behind my friends as we strode into sixth-hour.

I had a difficult time focusing in Spanish. As the numbness in my toes disappeared, tingling sensations shot through my feet.

By the end of class, the tingling was gone. My toes had returned to their normal color, except for my big toe, which had turned black and blue. Although my heels hurt, I slipped on my shoes and plodded to PE.

I caught a break when Mr. Mohr, one of the phy ed teachers, saw me limp into the locker room. "Now what did you do, Abrams? Take a tumble ice skating?"

"Wish I would've." I removed my shoes and showed him the blisters on my heels.

"You can't play volleyball with heels like that. Follow me into my office."

I soon left the noisy locker room with a library pass and a large bandage on each heel. While shuffling to the library, I stopped at my locker and grabbed my homework.

After finishing math, I reflected on the day's fire drill. I now understood why Principal Knox had us practice safety drills week after week. Even though our class had a sub, everyone knew what to do and left the building quickly and safely.

That evening, after working on social studies and English, I thought about the problems with my new shoes. Never again would I wear shoes that didn't fit, no matter how cool they looked.

I fished out my Rules of Never notebook from my desk drawer. I pulled out the blue pen stuck inside the wire loops and flipped opened the notebook to page six. On the top line I printed RULE SIX: "NEVER WEAR THE WRONG SIZE SHOES."

I closed the notebook, shoved the pen back inside the wire loops and returned the notebook to the drawer.

Before hitting the hay, I checked out my toes and hobbled over to my sock drawer. For the first time in a long while I wore socks to bed—thick woolen ones.

NEVER GO TO A DANCE FEELING QUEASY

House rules "rule" the house. My parents believed a clear set of rules was essential to a smooth-running household. By the time I had turned thirteen I lived with over forty rules, and every birthday the list grew by four or more.

My parents made sure I was aware of Rule 22, School Attendance. "Remember," they said over and over, "if you miss school for any reason, you'll be confined to the house. No exceptions."

√   √   √

I woke up Friday with a dull headache and sick to my stomach.

Why the morning of the Valentine's Day dance?

I crawled out of bed, shuffled into the bathroom and got ready for school in slow motion. After combing my hair, I grabbed my backpack and plodded down the stairs and into the kitchen.

"Do you want scrambled eggs for breakfast, Phil?" Mom asked, standing in front of the stove.

"Not hungry, Mom." I set my backpack on the island counter.

"You can't go to school on an empty stomach." Mom put on her grease-stained bib apron. "You must eat something. How about some French toast?"

"Can't. Stomach hurts."

"You, too?" Mom tied her apron around her waist. "Your father was grumbling about his stomach before he left to drop Kaylee at school. I hope the ham salad sandwiches I fixed last night weren't bad."

"What do you mean?"

"Wait a sec and I'll tell you." Mom went to the fridge and removed a package of ham. She opened it and sniffed the meat. "Omigosh."

"What's the matter?"

"The ham has a sour smell." Mom flipped over the package. "According to the expiration date, this ham should've been thrown out a week ago." She stepped over to the sink, tossed the meat down the disposal and washed her hands.

Mom turned and looked at me. "You might have a touch of food poisoning."

"Food poisoning? You're joking, right?"

"Afraid not."

Mom cast a worried look my way. "You're a little pale, Phil. Why don't you stay home from school?"

"I'll be okay," I said, not wanting to miss the dance I had eagerly waited for all week.

Mom placed her hand on my forehead. "You don't have a fever."

"See. I'll be fine."

"You shouldn't go to school hungry. At least have a piece of toast."

"No time. Gotta go or I'll miss the bus."

"Well, if you can't get through the day, call me at work and I'll come and get you." Mom handed me my winter jacket. "Bundle up, it's thirty-eight outside."

"Thanks, Mom." I threw on my jacket, snatched my backpack off the counter and set off to catch the bus. I met a shivering CJ at the end of his driveway.

"You okay, Phil?" CJ asked as we made our way to the bus stop. "You're moving kinda slow."

"Stomachache. I ate some rotten meat for dinner. Hope I make it through school. Don't wanna miss the dance."

"Skip school and come to the dance anyway."

"Can't. You know my parents and their 1000 rules."

"Oh, yeah. I forgot. Rule 22."

The cold, fresh air must've done some good, because when I arrived at the bus stop, my stomach had settled down.

The bus ride to school was uneventful, but by the end of first hour, I knew I should have stayed home. My head throbbed and my stomach churned.

My morning was miserable. Friends and teachers left me alone or suggested I go home. I spent lunch sitting in the library with my eyes closed and rubbing my pounding temples.

The afternoon classes were just as bad, and by the time the bus dropped me off, I felt even worse.

After I got home, I dragged myself upstairs to my room, undressed and crawled into bed. I slept until Mom called me for dinner.

When I woke up, I felt a bit better. I put on my sweats, headed down the stairs and walked into the kitchen.

"How you feeling, Phil?" Mom asked.

"Not great, but the nap helped."

"Where's Kaylee?" Dad asked, joining us.

"At a sleepover," Mom replied.

Moments later, my parents and I sat down to a meal of meatloaf, mashed potatoes and peas. Using my fork,

I speared a small slice of meat and set it on my plate.

"Phil, please pass the peas," Mom said.

I handed Mom the bowl, but before helping herself, she filled the serving spoon with peas and dumped them onto my plate.

"Really, Mom? You know I can't stand peas. Besides, aren't peas supposed to be green? Some are tan."

"Don't be so picky." Mom set the bowl on the table and spooned a helping of peas onto her plate.

Not knowing if I was even hungry, I cut off a small piece of meat and popped it into my mouth. But after swallowing the first morsel, I scratched the idea of eating anything else.

"No appetite, son?" Dad asked while dishing another helping of mashed potatoes onto his plate.

"Upset stomach."

"Me too. Had one all morning. Finally went away after lunch."

I pushed my plate away from me. "Dad, can I be excused? I need to lie down."

"Certainly. Hope you feel better."

I trudged upstairs, got ready for the dance and crawled onto the bed. I propped myself up against a mound of pillows and watched cartoons.

Twenty minutes later, the doorbell chimed. "Phil, Shane's here," Mom hollered from the foot of the stairs.

"Be right there." I dragged my body off the bed,

gave myself the once-over in the bathroom mirror and slogged down the stairs.

"Holy cow, Phil," Shane said, waiting for me in the entryway. "You look worse than you did at school."

"I feel as bad as I look."

"You gonna make it?" Shane zipped up his jacket.

"Yeah. I lasted through school. I can get through the dance."

"Well, whatever you do, don't puke in my dad's truck. He cleaned it after work."

"I'll try not to," knowing that was a real possibility. "Catch ya later, Mom," I hollered, slipping on my jacket. I shut the front door and lumbered over to the pickup parked in the driveway.

"Hi, Mr. Olson," I said, climbing into the back.

"Hey, Phil."

I collapsed back against the seat, hoping I didn't barf.

Shane's father cranked up the heater and backed out of the driveway. No one spoke during the ten-minute ride. I was relieved since I didn't want to talk to anyone.

"Okay, boys, have fun," Mr. Olson said, as he stopped in the school's parking lot near the front entrance. "By the way, Shane, what time do I come and get you?"

"Nine-thirty. And Dad, please don't forget like Tuesday's basketball practice."

"I won't, son. Meet you guys here at 9:30."

Shane and I stepped from the truck, peeled off our jackets and tossed them onto the passenger seat. As we closed the doors, his father put the truck into gear and gunned the engine. The sharp turn he made in the snow-covered parking lot caused the tires to squeal as he drove away.

Once Shane and I entered the packed gym, we quickly found CJ, Clara and a few other friends hanging out by the bleachers.

"Whaddaya doing here, Phil?" CJ asked.

"Hunting elephants. Whaddaya think?"

"I didn't mean it like that. Just surprised you came. In PE, you looked like my sister when she's gonna toss her cookies."

"No matter how bad I look, CJ, I still look better than you."

Shane and Clara chuckled.

"Hilarious, guys," CJ said.

I joined the conversation but chatted with friends for only a short time.

"Where ya headed, Phil?" Clara asked as I plodded up the bleachers. "Aren't ya going to ask Paris to dance? You've been eyeing her up for weeks. It's a slow dance and she's by herself." Clara pointed to Paris on the other side of the gym. "Go for it."

I turned and spotted Paris standing alone wearing a

pink sweatshirt with a NASA logo and faded jeans. She looked pretty as ever. "Love to, Clara, but my stomach's killing me."

"You aren't chicken, are you?"

"I'm not chicken. Just don't feel well."

"If you say so," Clara said as she turned and left.

For the next hour I sat in the bleachers and listened to my stomach gurgle.

Since I hadn't eaten all day, I was famished. I trudged down the bleachers, cut through the jam-packed dance floor and made my way to an exit.

I pushed open the double doors leading into the cafeteria. A bunch of kids sat in the lunchroom talking, munching on snacks or playing with their phones. I snaked my way through the tables and chairs to the vending machines at the far end of the room.

I bought a granola bar and an apple juice and took a seat. I devoured the bar and gulped down the juice. I was about to get up and head back to the gym when Paris and Nicole Gabinski, my science lab partner, stopped at my table.

"Hi, Phil," Nicole said.

"Hi, Nicole."

"I see you were hungry too," Nicole said, spotting the green wrapper and empty bottle on the table. "By the way, Phil, have you met my friend Paris?"

How lucky is this?

But as I stood to introduce myself, I threw up a little in my mouth. Instead of saying hi, I slapped my hand over my mouth and tore across the cafeteria, knocking over several chairs on the way.

I dashed into the boys' bathroom and darted into the closest stall. As I fell to my knees in front of the toilet, my stomach erupted. Puke spewed from my mouth like water from a fire hose, spraying the toilet, the floor, my jeans and my tennis shoes.

I knelt with my throat on fire, my eyes tearing up and my heart galloping a mile a minute. After a brief bout of dry heaves, I took three long, slow breaths to compose myself.

I gotta clean this up before I become known as 'Puker Phil.'

I wiped away the tears with my sleeve, stood and slid the metal latch to the locked position. Using wads of toilet paper, I brushed the puke from my jeans and shoes, cleaned the outside of the toilet bowl and sopped up the floor. I kept flushing the toilet to get rid of the smell. It didn't help.

When finished, I unlocked the door, eased it open and poked my head out. Seeing no one, I kicked off my shoes and climbed out of my jeans.

I stepped from the stall and hurried to the sink in my boxers and stocking feet. Using soap from the dispenser, I washed the front of my pants.

While hiking up my jeans, I noticed puke had seeped through to my boxers.

What next?

I zipped back into the stall, peeled off my pants and slipped out of my boxers. I cleaned myself up, yanked on my jeans and flushed the toilet.

I picked up my boxers like they were atomic waste and carefully rolled them up. I rushed from the stall and stashed the boxers at the bottom of a trash can.

Grabbing my shoes, I lathered them in soap, rinsed them off with hot water and wrung them out. I washed my hands and face, threw on my waterlogged shoes and scooted over to the hand dryers on the wall.

I stood between two blowers drying my jeans when Shane appeared from around the corner. "Holy smokes, Phil. Smells like a combo of fish guts, gym socks and urinal cakes."

"Funny, Shane. But this is no time to joke around. You won't believe what happened."

"Probably won't." Shane pinched his nose. "But make it fast before I pass out."

As I told Shane my story, he laughed so hard he had trouble catching his breath. When through laughing, he said, "Well, at least Paris will remember you."

"No kidding, but not in a good way."

"Yeah. You really messed that up."

"Right now, I have bigger problems than worrying about Paris. What am I gonna do? Can't go back into the gym."

"You got that right. You'll gross everyone out."

"What if I hide in the john until the dance is over?"

"Probably your best bet." Shane checked his phone. "My dad will be here in twelve minutes, so you won't hafta wait long."

"Promise you won't say a word to anyone about me puking."

"I won't say a word, but you owe me big time. See ya in twelve minutes." Shane headed off to the gym.

While blow-drying my jeans, I heard some guys about to enter the bathroom.

Just my luck.

I ducked into the farthest stall from the door and locked the door behind me. As the boys walked into the john, I scrambled on top of the toilet seat and stooped down, hoping they wouldn't see me.

"It reeks in here," said one of the boys as he approached the urinals in front of my stall.

I stared through the slit between the door and

the side of the stall and saw two boys. One was Ben something-or-other, and the second was Slate Harper, McKenzie's eighth-grade brother.

McKenzie was in my homeroom. The blabbermouth kept secrets for less time than it takes to cook a bowl of Minute Rice.

If Slate finds me, he'd tell his sister for sure.

"Smells like rotten eggs," Slate said, stepping up to the urinal.

"Rotten eggs don't smell this gross. This is gut-wrenching," Ben said. His raspy voice sounded like he had a cold.

"You're right about that." Slate unzipped his fly. "Let's take a wizz and get outta here."

"How come flies aren't made to close when you zip them down?" Ben asked. "Wouldn't it be easier?"

"Who cares? You know, Ben, at times you ask the dumbest questions."

Ben and Slate walked over to the sinks, washed their hands and appeared to leave. I relaxed. That's when I noticed, "Please seat yourself" scratched on the back of the stall door. I grinned.

Balancing on the toilet seat, I stretched my neck and peeked over the top of the stall. Both guys had left. I was safe, but as I stepped off the toilet, my foot slipped and plunged into the bowl.

I stared at my foot under three inches of water

and shook my head in disbelief.

Great. Just great.

I lifted my foot from the bowl, kicked off my tennis shoe and wrung it out over the toilet. Unlocking the stall, I went over to the sink and rinsed my shoe with hot water.

I wrung out my shoe, washed my hands and hobbled over to a hand dryer. As I stood drying my shoe, Shane dawdled into the bathroom.

"Where've you been, Shane?"

"I told you I'd be back in twelve minutes."

"Seemed longer than that."

Shane checked his phone. "Sixteen minutes to be exact, but it doesn't matter."

"Why not?"

"Cuz, I texted my dad and told him we'd be ten minutes late. By then most kids will have left."

"Good thinking, but he can't park in front of school. Someone might spot us."

"He's not. He's meeting us in the parking lot behind the gym."

"Sometimes, Shane, you're brilliant," I said, shoving my foot into my soggy shoe.

"I know. By the way, Phil, how ya feeling? You look a lot better."

"Barfing worked wonders. My stomachache and headache are gone, but my throat burns a little."

"Let's wait by the entrance where the smell isn't so bad," Shane suggested. "I'll act as lookout."

While we killed time, I told Shane about hiding in the stall and my foot slipping into the toilet. While Shane chuckled, his phone pinged.

"My dad's here." Shane tucked his phone in his pocket and poked his head around the corner. "The coast is clear. Let's go."

With Shane in the lead, we hustled down the half-lit hallway, my wet shoes sloshing with each step.

I followed Shane as he pushed through the double doors and stepped into the cold night. Shane scanned the parking lot. "Nobody's around."

"Let's motor," I said, crouching for protection against the biting wind.

We dashed over to the truck, and Shane yanked opened the front door. Instead of finding our coats, he found Rocky, his black lab, lying on the seat staring at us and wagging his tail. "Dad, where's our jackets?"

"Back seat. I figured you didn't want dog hair all over them."

Shane opened the back door and grabbed our jackets. We threw them on and climbed in.

"Buckled up?" Shane's father asked us.

"Yup," Shane and I replied in unison.

Mr. Olson put the truck in gear and sped off.

Although hot air blasted from the heater, I rolled

down the window a few inches. Two-thirds of the way home, Mr. Olson's nose twitched like a rabbit's. "Pee-yew. Did you fart, son?"

"No, Dad."

"Well, someone broke some serious wind."

"It was Rocky, Dad."

"Oh, yeah. Forgot about him." Mr. Olson partially rolled down his window.

Shane gave me his "I-saved-your-butt" look.

A short time later, we drove into my driveway. I closed the window and unbuckled my seat belt. "Thanks for the ride home, Mr. Olson."

"Anytime, Phil."

I threw open the door and stepped from the truck. "See ya later, Shane."

I climbed the front porch steps, hoping no one was home. I unlocked the door, quietly entered the house, flicked on the entryway lights and gently shut the door behind me.

I slipped out of my jacket and sniffed the sleeves. No smell, so I hung the jacket in the closet. I pulled off my shoes and socks, tiptoed to the end of the entryway and gave the house a quick once-over.

Even though the house was well lit, my parents appeared to be gone.

I grabbed my shoes, stuffed my socks inside and dashed across the floor to the stairs.

I flew up the stairs two at a time, snatched a garbage bag from the linen closet and zipped into the bathroom. I stripped, tossed my clothes and shoes into the bag and tightened the drawstring.

I turned on the shower full blast. Not waiting until the water turned warm, I jumped in. After showering, I toweled off, threw on some boxers and put on a T-shirt and sweatpants.

Starving, I grabbed the garbage bag from the bathroom and bounded down the stairs. After dropping my smelly clothes by the washing machine, I went into the kitchen and raided the fridge.

As I sat down to stuff myself, I saw Mom's sticky note on the table. "At neighbors playing cards. Back by eleven. Text me when home."

I texted Mom while gorging myself on leftover meatloaf. After guzzling down a huge glass of milk, I went upstairs and played video games. When I turned in for the night, my parents still weren't home.

I was too worried to fall asleep—not because of what Paris might think of me or that Shane would spill the beans about me barfing at the dance.

No, I was stressed out because of the boxers I had buried in the trash.

In other middle schools that's not a big deal, but our custodian did weird things with items he found. A month ago, he blacked out the names in a love letter and stapled it inside the lunch menu display case. Kids went crazy for days trying to figure out who the two lovebirds were.

Last week the custodian used a magic marker to circle the initial S on a grungy jock and hung it on a basketball trophy inside the school's trophy case. The attached note read: "Please claim at the custodian's office." Every guy at Lost Creek whose first or last name began with S endured tons of grief.

Which brings me back to my buried boxers. Ever since someone stole my gym shorts in second grade, my mother has printed ABRAMS inside my clothes. If the custodian found my branded boxers, no telling what he might do.

I lay in bed, picturing hordes of students gawking at the top of the flagpole in front of school. Below the American flag fluttered my puke-stained boxers.

After hours without sleep, I began yawning. As my eyelids drooped, I envisioned someone making out the large letters on the waistband. I fell asleep to a chant of: **ABRAMS! ABRAMS! ABRAMS! ABRAMS!**

When I awoke in the morning, I flopped back the covers, swung my legs over the side of the bed and stood. To my surprise, I felt fine.

"Phil, breakfast is ready," Mom called from the kitchen as I finished dressing.

"Be right there." I scooted down the stairs and into

the kitchen. The smell of fried bacon hung in the air.

"Smells great, Mom. What are we having?"

"Waffles and turkey bacon."

"Can't wait."

"Not surprised." Mom set a plate of extra-crispy bacon and a platter of waffles on the table and sat down. "You didn't eat a thing yesterday."

"Pigged out on leftover meatloaf before I went to bed," I said, taking my seat.

Shortly afterwards Dad joined us. The three of us enjoyed a breakfast of waffles, topped with strawberries and whipped cream, bacon and orange juice.

"How was the dance, Phil?" Dad asked, grabbing two bacon strips. "Have a good time?"

"Not really." I told my parents what had happened. I spared them the parts about slipping off the toilet seat and making a lousy impression on Paris.

"Sorry to hear that, Phil," Mom said, drizzling syrup over her waffle. "I know you were looking forward to the dance."

"Well, it's over. Plus, I learned a valuable lesson last night."

Dad took a loud sip of coffee and set the cup on the table. "And what might that be?"

"Never go to a dance feeling queasy."

My parents looked at one another and chuckled.

RULE EIGHT

NEVER FORGET TO TAKE A LEAK BEFORE CLASS

Health class at Lost Creek Middle School was anything but healthy.

Students were required to take health for two twelve-week sessions. Kids endured a session in sixth grade and suffered through another one in seventh. That meant I had Terrance William Fry, the worst teacher in the solar system—again.

Like an antique lamp, Mr. Fry was a fixture at Lost Creek. He had taught health in the same room and had sat behind the same desk for nearly half a century. Kids joked he had taught George Washington.

For a health teacher, Mr. Fry certainly didn't look the part. His egg-shaped head was bald, and the top half of his chubby face was wrinkled like the bark on an old oak tree. A thicket of white hair sprouted out of his ears and two bushy eyebrows met above his crooked nose. A scruffy mustache and a thick beard hid the bottom half of his face.

The teacher weighed more than a sumo wrestler, moved as fast as a glacier and was wider than he was tall. Years earlier, students had started calling him "Wide Track" and the name stuck.

Walking into Wide Track's classroom was like stepping into a dreary basement. Because the room once served as a planetarium, the walls and the ceiling tiles had been painted black.

The "Gloom and Doom" room, as kids called it, lacked any personal touch. No inspirational posters. No vibrant artwork. No catchy sayings.

Even the bulletin board on the front wall remained bare except for a thick layer of dust. Oh, four rusty thumbtacks were still stuck there, and if one looked closely, one saw an abandoned cobweb.

The room's décor wasn't the reason students disliked health. It was Wide Track himself. First, he believed in lots of homework. He assigned three to four worksheets each day, including Friday.

Second, Wide Track refused to use technology in

class. He saw no need for educational apps, online homework or Chromebooks. The Smart Board looked new because no one had ever written on it. A PowerPoint to him was for plugging in a toaster.

His wicked temper was the third reason kids didn't care for Mr. Fry. Students won a good tongue-lashing or got "Fryed" for countless offenses. Even trivial infractions set him off. Kids were Fryed for such misdeeds as coming late to class, forgetting a red pen or chewing gum.

The fourth reason students disliked Wide Track was his strict restroom policy. Lost Creek teachers frowned on kids visiting the restroom during class. They preferred we use the bathroom between classes or during lunch.

A few teachers employed a seven-minute rule. Students could use the restroom only during the first and last seven minutes of class.

But whether the teachers had a seven-minute rule or not, in an emergency, students were allowed to leave. Not the heartless Mr. Fry, who didn't consider the dire need to take a leak a crisis.

Like last Tuesday, a day Drew Meyer and his classmates have seared into their memories.

Drew had recently moved into the school district. Short for a thirteen-year-old, the first thing one noticed about Drew was the big ears jutting out on either side of his head. Rumors spread around school he could track down every little sound. Drew soon acquired the nickname Radar.

Following Wide Track's dull lecture on "How to Take Charge of Your Health," four worksheets were passed out. After everyone had the assignment, Wide Track cleared his throat. "Any questions?"

Radar, who sat in the first desk two rows over, raised his hand.

Wide Track pushed aside the clutter on his desk and lifted a corner of his calendar. He peeked under it, studied the seating chart and set his calendar back down.

The teacher eyed Radar over the rim of his glasses that had inched down his nose. "What is it, Geyer?"

"It's Meyer, sir."

"Whatever. What is it, Meyer?"

"Can I go to the restroom?" Radar asked, his tone urgent.

Wide Track rested his elbows on the calendar and glared at Radar for a few moments before speaking. "No, you may not. I clearly explained my classroom rules the first day of health. Under no circumstance will a student leave class to visit the restroom. Doesn't anyone listen anymore?"

"I moved here a week and a half ago," Radar said, fidgeting in his desk. "How was I supposed to know you can't use the bathroom during class? At my old school, teachers let us leave."

"This is not your old school." Wide Track dug a white handkerchief out of his pants pocket. "Now get to work." The teacher blew his nose and inspected the gob of snot in the hanky. He folded the hanky in half and slipped it back into his pocket.

Figuring the face-off between Wide Track and Radar was over, I opened my textbook. I turned to the chapter titled "Tobacco and Its Effects."

As I answered the first question on worksheet one, I caught a glimpse of Radar out of the corner of my eye. He kept raking his fingers through his thick, straw-colored hair, tapping his feet and glancing at the clock on the wall behind the teacher's desk.

Radar has a major problem.

I moved onto the second question.

With two minutes left in class, I checked on Radar. He sat rubbing his hands on his jeans and his foot-tapping had increased. By the painful expression on his face, I assumed his bladder was ready to burst.

Suddenly, Radar wildly waved both hands above his head, trying to capture Wide Track's attention.

The teacher slid his glasses down the bridge of his nose. "What is it now, Geyer, um, Meyer?" Wide Track asked without bothering to hide his irritation.

Radar sprang to his feet and stood beside his desk, startling classmates and the teacher. "Can I go to the restroom, Mr. Fry?" Radar pleaded. "I gotta go bad."

Wide Track glowered at Radar. "Need I remind you of the rule? No one leaves my room except in an emergency. Now get to—"

"This is an emergency, Mr. Fry. If I don't get to the john, I'll pee my pants."

Wide Track's eyes narrowed and his lips tightened. "It's called a restroom, not a john, Meyer, and keeping your jeans dry is not my concern."

Wide Track glanced at his watch. "I will, however, grant you two concessions because you are new. You may remain standing and you may leave the room first."

Radar collected his health materials and stood alongside his desk with his legs crossed.

Wanting to see how this played out, I shoved my worksheets into my assignment folder. I zipped up my binder and turned my attention to Radar.

Radar's usual confident expression had left his face. Instead he wore a look of desperation. With each passing tick of the clock, he seemed more distressed.

Five seconds before the bell, two historic events happened in health at the same time. The class started a countdown and Wide Track let it proceed.

"Five," the class shouted.

Sweat trickled down Radar's forehead.

"Four."

Radar chewed his bottom lip.

"Three." Kids seated in the back rows stood.

Radar rocked back and forth.

"Two," the class shouted louder.

Radar glanced sideways at me, his face flushed with panic.

"One," the class roared.

The bell rang and Radar rocketed from the room. As he flew through the doorway, he turned too sharply and smacked the back of his hand against the door.

"Ow!" he cried out as his textbook, notebook and pens went flying. Radar didn't hesitate. He left everything where it lay and tore down the hallway.

On my way out of the room, I gathered Radar's materials and waited for him by the lockers across from the restroom.

"I cut that close," Radar said as he approached me, looking relieved. "I'm glad the restroom was nearby. If I had peed my jeans, I'd never live it down."

"Probably not." I handed him his textbook, notebook and pens.

"Thanks for getting my stuff, Phil." Radar wiped off the grimy footprint on the notebook onto his jeans. "I owe you one."

"No problem," I said, not telling him our classmates almost trampled me to death stampeding from health class to get to lunch. "How's your hand?"

"I'll live." Radar tried to shake the pain from his hand. "That's on Fry. I can't believe he doesn't let anyone go to the john."

"There's countless things about Wide Track I don't believe. But look at the bright side."

"What do you mean 'bright side?' I almost peed my pants," Radar said as we worked our way to our lockers to ditch our books.

"Well, first of all, we have one less health class. Only thirty-nine of those snoozers left, but who's counting?"

Radar chuckled.

"Second, you made a boring class exciting. That's the most fun I've had in health since a sixth grader barfed on Wide Track's desk. Even Martha, the biggest killjoy in seventh grade, joined in the countdown."

"Glad you and Martha found my misery amusing." Radar cracked a smile.

"And third, you taught me and probably the rest of the class a meaningful lesson."

"What's that?"

"You'll find out tomorrow."

The following day, before health class, the boys' john near Wide Track's room was jam-packed. I assumed the girls' restroom was crammed too.

NEVER BET MONEY YOU DON'T HAVE

Wide Track ran health class with military precision.

Each day, Wide Track's mission was to complete a lesson in fifty minutes. No discussions, guest speakers or hands-on learning held up his objective. At no time did he allow spontaneity or fun to creep into his classroom.

His class schedule never varied. At 10:44 AM, the bell rang announcing the start of class. After students plunked down in their desks, Wide Track promptly took attendance.

Forty seconds later, Wide Track rose from his chair and huffed and puffed his way to the door. That was our signal to stand and face the American flag hanging on the side wall.

Following Wide Track's lead, we placed our right hands over our hearts and recited the "Pledge of Allegiance."

After saying the pledge, students slid back into their desks while Wide Track closed the door and made his way to his chair at a snail's pace.

At precisely 10:46, a boring forty-eight-minute class began. For the first eleven minutes, we corrected and handed in our homework.

Assignments were done on time, or else. They counted one-half the final grade and being caught with unfinished work got the student Fryed.

Beginning at 10:57, students took notes from a reading or a lecture. Because Wide Track read or talked a hundred miles an hour, note-taking was a challenge.

A half hour later, three or four worksheets were passed out. Students spent the remaining seven minutes of class working on their assignment.

Wide Track never left his cushioned chair to help anyone, and we were all too afraid to ask him a question. Since there was never enough time to finish the worksheets, I had homework every night.

The only interruptions to Wide Track's daily routine were when he showed a DVD, which was rare, or gave a test. Every other Friday, we took a twenty question true-or-false test on our notes. The combined six test scores counted half our final grade.

√   √   √

After another long tedious class, Shane, CJ, Clara and I discussed health while chowing down lunch.

"Health is the boringest class in the world," Clara said, as she poked a fork at her spaghetti. "The class sucks the life out of you."

CJ, Shane and I nodded.

"No one can make health exciting," CJ said while twirling strands of spaghetti around his fork.

"I can," I blurted out too quickly.

"Yeah, right." CJ peered at me like I had just swallowed the school mascot. "How are ya gonna do that?"

"Wide Track thinks he's always right, I'll prove him wrong," I said without thinking. I tore off part of a bun and popped the chunk into my mouth.

"You don't have the guts," Shane said. "I dare ya to do it."

"I'll double dare ya," CJ added and stuffed a forkful of pasta into his mouth.

Stung by Shane's lack of guts comment, I said, "What's in it for me?"

"You'll be the talk of the whole school. You'll become a legend," CJ said through a mouthful of spaghetti.

"Not good enough. Let's make a bet."

"Great idea," Shane said.

"It's gotta be worth something." I speared two greasy meatballs with my fork. "Wide Track freaks out when anyone disagrees with him. I'll get Fryed for sure."

"How about money?" Shane asked.

My ears perked up. "How much we talking?" I crammed the meatballs into my mouth.

"What if we each chip in ten bucks?" Shane asked.

CJ and Clara peered at Shane as though he had lost his marbles.

"That's… that's a lot of money," CJ sputtered. Flecks of pasta peppered the table. "Too rich for me."

"Gross, CJ," Clara said.

"Oops." CJ wiped the table alongside his tray with his napkin.

"What about you, Clara?" Shane asked as he cut spaghetti strands into small pieces with his knife. "You in?"

Clara shook her head. "I can't afford that either, Shane. I'm saving for a new phone."

"C'mon, guys. Phil's all talk." Shane paused for a few seconds. "Tell you what. I'm so confident Phil will chicken out, I'll throw in twenty bucks if you each toss in five."

"I don't know, Shane," CJ said, balancing a meatball on his knife and slowly inching both toward his mouth.

"Neither do I," Clara chimed in while watching CJ.

Inches from CJ's mouth, the meatball toppled off the knife and onto his tray.

"Nice try, CJ," Clara said. "Why don't you just use your fork?"

"What's the fun in that?" CJ set the meatball back on his knife and started over.

As Shane tried to persuade Clara and CJ to go in with him, I mulled over the bet. The wager was risky, but if I won, I could pay off the debt I owed my sister. She had been nagging me for weeks for the twenty bucks she had loaned me. The other ten I'd spend on myself.

Though leery about losing even five bucks, Clara and CJ agreed to the new terms. "Okay, the three of us are in, Phil," Shane said. "Are you?"

I chugged the rest of my milk. "Yup."

Shane and I knocked knuckles to seal the bet.

"It's gotta be done tomorrow," Shane said.

"No sweat." I stood, pushed in my chair, dropped off my tray and walked back to our table. "Catch you guys in math."

"Where ya headed, Phil?" CJ asked as his greasy meatball fell off his knife for the second time.

"Outside. Need some fresh air."

"Fresh air ain't gonna help you tomorrow," Shane said. "You're gonna need CPR after you lose the bet."

"I'll say," CJ added.

Clara remained silent.

"No sly comment, Clara?" I asked.

A devilish look came into Clara's eyes. "The only thing I have to say, Phil, is this." She whispered so softly I barely heard what she was saying.

I leaned over the table and pressed my ear close to her to catch every word.

"You have pasta sauce on your chin," she said loud enough that kids eating at tables near us heard her. My friends cracked up.

"You guys are hilarious." I grabbed Clara's napkin, quickly wiped my chin clean and tossed the napkin on the table. "You won't be laughing when I win thirty bucks."

I stormed off down the hallway, pushed open a door to the playground and went outside to mull over the bet.

How was I pulling this off? Me and my big mouth.

The next morning, Shane spied me heading to English. "Hey, Phil. Don't forget our bet." He marched up to me and playfully punched me in the shoulder.

I gave Shane a friendly shove. "Got my thirty bucks?"

"A third of it is right here." Shane patted his jeans pocket. "Clara paid me coming into school, and CJ gave me five ones a minute ago."

"Let's see it."

"What? You don't believe me?" Shane reached in his pocket and hauled out a small wad of crumpled money. "See. Ten bucks."

"Where's the rest?" I asked.

"In a safe place. Where's your money?"

"At home. I don't plan on losing."

"Hope you're good for it. I've already made plans for my share." Shane gave me a goofy grin.

"Make sure you keep the money safely tucked in your pocket until health," I fired back.

"Why?" Shane asked, as we strode into English together.

"Cuz, you'll be paying me right after class."

"Wanna bet? Oh, yeah. We already have a wager." Shane chuckled, but I ignored his feeble attempt to be funny.

I spent English, science and social studies worrying about the bet. As I slid into my desk in health, Shane walked by. "Good luck, man."

"Won't need it," I calmly replied, hiding my true feelings. I was as nervous as a worm in a robin's nest.

I didn't have money to buy a pack of gum, much less thirty bucks to pay my friends. I had to win the bet.

But how?

"Get out your worksheets," Wide Track instructed after getting comfy in his brown leather chair.

After we corrected and turned in our homework, Wide Track picked up a pamphlet titled *Health News* from his desk. While he read the pamphlet, we took notes on middle schoolers' eating habits.

When done, Wide Track set the pamphlet on his desk, adjusted his glasses and looked out at his bored class. "As you see by the article, middle schoolers eat too much sodium, drink too much soda and consume too much sugar."

I peeked at the wall clock behind Wide Track's desk: 11:14. Twenty minutes to make something happen. My palms began to sweat.

Wide Track reached down and hauled out a beat-up book from his desk drawer. I winced when I noticed the title *Nutrition for Kids*.

A faded yellow envelope, acting as a bookmark, was inserted in the middle of the book. "Let's go over some nutritious options to junk food." Wide Track opened the book to the marked page and spewed out healthful substitutes.

I furiously scribbled notes on alternatives to junk food like popcorn, dried fruit, oatmeal and yogurt. When done, we moved on to what comprises a healthy eating plate.

After what seemed an eternity, Wide Track returned the envelope to the page and closed his book.

I checked the clock: 11:27. In seven minutes I was out thirty bucks. I stole a glance at Shane. He clutched his throat with his hands.

I need a miracle.

While biting my thumbnail, it hit me. I frantically flicked through yesterday's notes.

"Before I hand out homework, are there any questions?" Wide Track's eyes darted back and forth across the room. He looked shocked when I raised my hand.

"What is it, Abrams?" Wide Track asked, the ceiling lights shining off his bald head.

I swallowed hard. "Mr. Fry, didn't you say yesterday a healthy eating plate included grains?"

"Yes, I did, Abrams. I also mentioned them a few minutes ago as part of a healthy meal."

"Well, Mr. Fry, I don't believe you did." I tried to steady my shaky voice. "I don't have anything about grains in today's notes."

Wide Track gave me a threatening look. "You're mistaken, Abrams." The teacher reopened his book and turned to the page he had just read. He ran his index finger slowly down the page until he found the sentence he wanted.

"It's right here at the beginning of the third paragraph," Wide Track snapped. "'A healthy eating plate includes vegetables, fruits, grains and foods high in protein.'" He stopped reading, lowered his book and looked me straight in the eye.

Both my knees shook and my heart raced, but I plunged ahead. I gulped, not at all confident I was right. "I be…b—lieve it's on the page, Mr. Fry, but you skipped grains when you read the sentence." I rubbed the sweat from my forehead.

Wide Track bristled at my remark. "I know what I read, Abrams." The teacher slapped his book shut and slammed it down so hard his desk shook.

"You're mis—mistaken, Mr. Fry," I stammered. Goosebumps ran up and down my bare arms.

"That's absurd." Wide Track's eyes flashed with anger.

Radar's hand shot up.

"What is it, Meyer?" the teacher barked, his ears and cheeks now a bright red.

"Phil is right, Mr. Fry. You forgot grains. I don't have them in my notes either."

"Neither do I," Jennifer Davis called out.

I couldn't believe my ears. I turned my head and saw Davis, who hadn't spoken to me since the first day of school, with her hand up.

What was Davis doing? Maybe Little Miss Dressed in Black wasn't so bad after all.

I smiled at her.

She sneered back.

So much for that idea.

Seeing I had found two allies, Wide Track pulled his glasses down to the tip of his nose and glared at the class over the rim. His eyes burned with anger, and the veins on his forehead throbbed.

We're gonna get Fryed.

Wide Track hesitated for a moment and stroked his beard as if thinking. He then did something so stunning and so out of character, students will talk about it for years.

His chair loudly creaked as the teacher leaned forward. "Let's take a poll," Wide Track said to the class in an almost pleasant manner. "By a show of hands, how many of you don't have grains written in today's notes?"

Every student raised a hand.

The teacher paused as if collecting his thoughts. "I guess I made a mistake."

Twenty-five students gasped and looked at each

other in bewilderment.

As Wide Track returned his book to the drawer, the bell rang for lunch.

No homework for the first time this year.

All of us stood to leave, but Wide Track barked, "Sit down. I haven't handed out your assignment."

Mutterings of disappointment filled the room as we plunked back down.

Radar, Jennifer and I passed out the worksheets. After everyone had three, Wide Track said, "You may now leave."

"Unbelievable, Phil," CJ said, coming up behind me in the hallway.

"Tell me about it. My legs feel like Jello."

"And what's with Davis? She can't stand ya."

"Beats me, but I'm glad she spoke up."

Shane and Clara caught up with us seconds later. "I sat at the edge of my seat waiting for you to get Fryed," Shane said. "Instead, Wide Track admits he made a mistake."

"Incredible," Clara chimed in.

Classmates from health hurrying past me gave me a thumbs-up or slapped me a high-five. Others hollered, "Awesome" or "Way to go, Abrams."

"That'll teach you guys to bet against me," I boasted. "Now, Shane, fork over thirty bucks."

Shane reached in his back pocket and pulled out

his wallet. He flipped it open and dug out a five and ten crinkled ones. "Here."

I snatched the fifteen dollars out of his hand. "Where's the rest?"

"I never dreamed you'd go through with it. I'll pay you the rest tomorrow. Promise."

"You better." I stuffed the money in my jeans pocket.

The four of us dumped our books in our lockers, grabbed our brown bags and headed to lunch.

As I lumbered into the cafeteria, I spied Radar standing at the end of the lunch line. I went over and tapped him on the shoulder.

Radar turned around. "Hey, Phil."

"Thanks for backing me up in class," I told him.

"I owed you one for picking up my books."

"Well, you're a lifesaver. Thanks again." I left and made a mental note to thank Davis for sticking her neck out for me.

When I find the courage.

I found CJ and Shane sitting at our usual table. Within seconds, Clara joined us. "You know, Phil, you're the talk of the cafeteria."

"I kinda got that by the stares I'm getting."

"Your fifteen minutes of fame," CJ said.

During lunch, friends and classmates dropped by and gave me pats on the back, high-fives and fist bumps. Congrats continued in my afternoon classes and on the bus ride home.

The next morning, Shane paid off the bet and health class returned to its lifeless way.

√   √   √

Three weeks later, I completed health. Even though class was a waste of time, I gained one useful insight and learned a valuable lesson.

A month earlier, I discovered I had been reciting the Pledge of Allegiance wrong. When I said the pledge, I stood, put my hand over my heart and proclaimed, "I pledge allegiance to the flag of the United States of America, and to the republic for Richard Stands, one nation under God, indivisible, with liberty and justice for all."

For years, I didn't understand who Richard Stands was, and what he had to do with the pledge.

One morning, while our class recited the pledge, Wide Track stumbled over the words. We stopped and started again.

This time the teacher slowly said the pledge. When he came "to the republic for Richard Stands," I realized the words were "to the republic for which it stands." Mystery solved.

I also learned a life lesson: Never bet money you don't have.

NEVER BACK DOWN FROM A BULLY

I strolled into second-hour science pumped. I had aced my first-hour spelling test, had no English homework and today was lab, which was always a fun time.

Science was my favorite subject and the main reason was the teacher, Mr. Pittman. He had taught at Lost Creek for over three decades, had a nerdy passion for science and was supercool.

The teacher never took himself too seriously and enjoyed making fun of himself. For instance, when class dragged, he played his guitar and sang a silly science ditty he had composed. He didn't play the guitar or sing well and by the end of the first verse, kids begged him to stop. Of course, he kept performing, making us plead even more.

Other times, he told us a funny story or attempted a yo-yo trick that never worked.

Mr. Pittman also wore a hat that complemented each lesson. He slipped on a chef's hat when showing us how to make a ketchup and vinegar volcano. While we studied fossil fuels, the teacher threw on a miner's hat. He wore a colorful propeller hat when teaching us about wind energy.

Today, the teacher stood by his workstation wearing a pink "Dentists Have Fillings Too" T-shirt and a light blue scrub cap with smiling teeth printed on it.

After taking attendance, Mr. Pittman slipped on his chemical-splattered lab coat, turned and faced us. "Let's get this show on the road."

The teacher reached into the inner pocket of his lab coat and pulled out a frog hand puppet. "Class, say hi to Ernie." Mr. Pittman adjusted Ernie's goggles.

"Hi, Ernie," the class said together.

"Good morning, fellow scientists," Ernie said in a high, squeaky voice. "Hey, did you hear the one about the invisible man marrying the invisible woman?"

Ernie paused for a moment, letting the words sink in. "Their kids were nothing to look at."

Nearly everybody groaned.

"Enough with the jokes, Ernie," Mr. Pittman said, eyeballing the frog. "We have an experiment to do."

The teacher's eyes swept over his audience. "Now that introductions are done, let me explain the experiment. You will determine if soda, tea, juice or water stain teeth."

Ernie twisted his head and stared at the teacher. "Water stains teeth?"

Mr. Pittman gazed at Ernie. "You should know the answer by now, Ernie. You and I have done this gig for years."

The class laughed.

Mr. Pittman and Ernie looked out over their attentive audience. "When you stain your teeth, you wear away the enamel, which protects the tooth's inner part," the teacher explained.

"Thanks for the explanation," Ernie chimed in.

The teacher glared at Ernie. "May I continue?"

"Sure. Just don't bore the kids to death." A smattering of chuckles rippled through the audience.

Mr. Pittman gave Ernie the stink eye and addressed the class. "Since we can't pull out anyone's teeth, we will use hard-boiled eggs instead."

Ernie gave Mr. Pittman a quizzical look. "Why hard-boiled eggs?"

"I'm getting to that, Ernie," the teacher said.

Nicole, a science whiz and my lab partner, cut in. "I can answer the question, Mr. Pittman."

"Okay, Nicole, but wait a sec." Mr. Pittman put Ernie back in his coat pocket, dragged over a wooden stool and sat down. "Go ahead, Nicole."

"Eggshells are similar to tooth enamel. The shell protects the egg and the enamel protects your teeth," Nicole explained to the class. "They also have a similar color."

"Couldn't have said it better myself, Nicole. Well done." Mr. Pittman stood, smoothed out his lab coat and snatched a pile of papers from a corner of his workstation. He handed them to me. "Pass these out, Phil. One sheet per table."

After I distributed the handouts, Mr. Pittman held up a copy. "Every table have a handout?" The teacher scanned the classroom, making sure each lab station had one. "Before beginning your experiment, you'll need to get your materials."

Mr. Pittman pointed at two long tables. One was loaded with beverages and the other was crammed with supplies. "One person will grab four plastic cups, four eggs and an eight-inch strip of masking tape. The other

person will get a soda, a bottle of juice and a bottle of tea."

The teacher plopped down on the stool. "After gathering your materials, follow the instructions on the handout. Questions?"

"Where do we get the water?" Clara asked from the middle of the room.

"From the faucets in back," the teacher replied.

"What if I crack an egg?" CJ asked.

"Thanks for the reminder, CJ," Mr. Pittman said. "Class, one other thing. If you split open the shell, the egg must be replaced. A cracked shell alters the experiment's results. Please be careful. I only have two extra eggs per class."

Mr. Pittman opened his mouth to say something else. But before he uttered another word, the classroom door flew open with such force the door smacked the wall behind it. Everyone's head swiveled to see Noah Fleming swagger through the doorway.

Terror swept over me like a giant tidal wave.

What was Fleming doing here? He was supposed to be in Indiana.

Fleming was nicknamed Moose because of his size and strength. He weighed more than a cement truck, was strong as an ox and had more hair on his chest than I had on my head.

Dumber than a houseplant, Moose spent most of

last year tormenting classmates, especially me. Of the ten worst qualities of a human, Moose had eleven of them.

The bully hated me and I hated him. He had done a number of cruel and embarrassing things to me in sixth grade.

So late last year, I evened the score a bit during gym. I soaked the crotch of his jeans with water, making it appear he had wet his pants. His friends teased him for days. Moose blamed his pals, but of course, they denied it.

The bus driver had kicked Moose off our bus on the last day of school for dangling his rear end out a window. As Moose stood in the parking lot, I poked my head out a window and yelled I had soaked his blue jeans.

Moose vowed to get even, but I wasn't worried. Since his family was moving out of state, I'd never see him again.

I was wrong.

"Welcome, Mister Fleming," Mr. Pittman said. "I heard you might be joining us today."

"You remember me?" Moose handed the teacher an admit slip.

"After the ruckus you caused last year outside my room, how could I forget you?"

"Wasn't my fault. The guy bumped into me, but

you sent me to the office."

"I sent you to the office because you slammed him into a locker."

"Whatever," Moose muttered back.

"Here." The teacher gave Moose the handout for the experiment. "I'll assign you a seat tomorrow. For now, Noah, you can work with Jenna and Bill. Kids, put up your hands."

Both raised their hands. By the glum expression on their faces, neither was thrilled having Moose as a lab partner.

"Didn't you move to Indiana?" Mr. Pittman asked Moose as the bully walked past him.

"Yeah, but my old man got transferred back." The bully glanced at the handout, crumpled up the paper and stuffed it into his jeans pocket.

As Moose strutted by my table, he stopped, bent over and jabbed his finger in my face. "You're in for a serious butt kicking, Abrams," the bully said, dropping his voice so Mr. Pittman didn't hear him. "I haven't forgotten what you did to my jeans."

I looked away, my eyes glued on a colorful poster hanging from the ceiling: "Books Can Take You Anywhere." At that moment, I wanted a book to take me home.

Mr. Pittman refocused the class as Moose made his way to his seat. "Let's get to work. Make sure you follow the handout to the letter."

The room became a bustle of activity. Nicole collected the cups, eggs and masking tape. I grabbed the juice, tea and soda.

While Nicole cut the masking tape into four equal pieces, I went to fill a cup with water. While standing in line, I stole a peek at Moose.

The bully sat next to Jenna, bouncing his pencil off the table while she labeled the cups. By his bored expression, he had no intention of helping with the experiment.

When Moose noticed me looking at him, he glared at me and snapped his pencil in two. I quickly filled the cup two-thirds full and gave Moose a wide berth while heading back to my lab station.

I didn't risk another peek at Moose. But I felt his beady eyes boring holes in the back of my head the rest of the period.

Nicole and I were wiping soda off our table when the bell rang. "For the next five days, you'll check your eggs and write your observations in your lab book," Mr. Pittman told the class.

As I tossed our wet paper towels into the trash, I checked on Moose. He flashed me a gonna-get-you-back smile. I quickly gathered my books and joined the line exiting the room.

Moose pushed back his chair and muscled his way

through a wall of students to the front of the room. He took a spot right behind me as the class filed from the room. When I neared the door, he shoved me so hard I stumbled forward into the hallway.

"Knock it off, Moose," I hollered, after regaining my footing.

"A taste of what's to come, Abrams," Moose said in mocking amusement. He faked a punch that caused me to flinch. The bully chuckled.

"Pick on someone your own size," Clara hollered, coming up from behind us.

"You have girls fight your battles now, Abrams?" Moose sneered at Clara. "Catch you two later."

The bully hiked up his jeans, pivoted and stomped down the hallway, now swarming with kids. They scattered like a herd of zebras running from a lion as the bully strutted past them.

"Thanks," I told Clara.

"You're welcome," Clara said as we headed to social studies. "Don't worry about Moose, Phil. He's nothing but a slimebucket."

"I know, but how ironic is this?"

"Whaddaya mean?"

"Remember the word of the day in English?"

"Wretched," Clara said.

"Recall what it means?"

"Miserable."

"Well, that sums up the rest of my school year."

Though Moose had been assigned to Ms. Joyner's homeroom, he seldom showed up. And because the bully had enrolled so late in the school year, his class schedule was different from mine. I only saw him in science and at lunch.

√   √   √

I managed to stay out of Moose's crosshairs for over a week, but my luck didn't hold. I was running late to social studies when Moose charged from the bathroom. I swerved to miss him, but he took a step in my direction, causing me to barrel into him.

"Watch where you're going, dork," Moose barked.

"Whatever, Moose," I said, unsure he heard me. Talking to him was like talking to a doorknob.

Hearing the commotion, Moose's two hefty pals, Snake and Stump, tore out of the bathroom and joined us. Jacob, known as Snake, and Derrick, known as Stump, were identical twins.

Nicknamed the Beef Brothers, both were as dumb as Moose. Classmates used to say the Beef Brothers shared a brain, but you never knew which one had it on any given day.

Moose poked his finger into my ribs.

"Ouch! Cut it out."

"Sorry. Did I poke you too hard?" By the look on Moose's face, he wasn't sorry at all. Instead, he looked pleased with himself.

My hand curled into a fist. I wanted to wipe that smug grin off his face, but if I threw one punch, Moose would beat the snot out of me.

"Let's go, Moose. We'll be late for PE," Snake said.

"So what?" Moose wiped his nose with the back of his meaty hand.

"Remember what Mohr told us last week," Stump added. "If we're late one more time, we get detention."

"Okay, guys. Don't get your undies in a bundle."

Moose ruffled my hair. "Later, Abrams." The bully belched in my face, turned and took off for PE with Stump and Snake by his side.

I followed the blockheads, but kept my distance.

"Whadda gutless wonder," Moose said loud enough so I heard his comment.

"Yeah," Stump bellowed. "Abrams doesn't live in a house, he lives in a chicken coop."

"Cluck. Cluck. Cluck," Moose squawked.

Moose and his pals walked down the hallway laughing.

I had a choice. Flee into social studies and be a coward for the rest of my life or stand up to the bully. Confronting Moose was a recipe for disaster. He had forearms bigger than my thighs. I had as much chance of beating up Moose as I did of acing an English test.

I made my decision.

"Thanks for nothing, buttface," I yelled before my courage vanished.

Moose froze in his tracks and spun on his heels. A hateful smile crossed his lips as he flexed his muscle-packed arms. The bully stormed toward me with Snake and Stump in tow.

Moose halted when we stood eyeball to eyeball. The Beef Brothers parked themselves behind Moose with their jaws set and their hands balled into fists, ready to fight.

"What did you say, Abrams?" the bully snarled through clenched teeth.

"Deck him, Moose." Stump pounded his fist into the palm of his hand. "And let's get outta here."

"You deaf, Moose?" I repeated the four words. I pronounced each syllable as if talking to a first grader. "Thanks—for—noth—ing—butt—face."

Moose stepped back and stared at me wide-eyed with his mouth hung open.

"Do I need to spell *buttface* for you?"

Moose's eyes grew wild and the veins in his neck bulged out like they were going to pop. He took a menacing step toward me.

With a hand the size of a first baseman's glove, Moose grabbed the front of my African Safari T-shirt that had a picture of three giraffes. "It's gonna be fun punching your lights out."

He was tearing me to pieces anyway, so I pressed on. "You know, Moose, you might wanna try Tic Tacs. While you're at it, take care of that forest of nose hair."

Moose tightened his vice-like grip on my T-shirt, his face contorted with anger.

"Don't squeeze the giraffes too tight," Snake said. "They might poop on your hand." Moose and his pals cracked up.

When the bully quit laughing, he took a quick look up and down the hallway, making sure no one was around.

"Payback time, Abrams." Moose hoisted me in the air with one hand, took three short steps with his tree-trunk legs and tossed me down the hallway like a bowling ball. I slid down the corridor with my back and butt cleaning the dirty floor. My journey ended when I crashed into a locker.

"Strike!" Moose yelled.

I lay spread-eagled on my back with my eyes closed and in a world of hurt. When I opened my eyes, my head was swimming.

With my vision blurred, the only things I could recognize were Moose's belly laugh, my rattling teeth and a spinning ceiling.

I struggled to sit up. I flexed my fingers, hands and wrists to check if anything was broken. While rubbing the back of my head searching for bumps, I noticed a sizable dent in a locker.

"Now you've done it, Abrams." Moose stared at me. "You're gonna hafta pay to fix the locker." The Beef Brothers, standing on either side of Moose, appeared amused.

Moose checked the hallway clock. "I guess we get detention."

"Ah, who cares." Snake scratched his butt.

"Yeah," Stump agreed. "Watching Abrams slide along the floor like a hockey puck is worth it."

"Now we're even, Abrams." Moose gave me a triumphant grin.

Moose and his pals slapped each other high-fives and clomped down the hallway, their footsteps echoing in the empty corridor. I glared at the back of their heads until they turned the corner.

I climbed to my feet, dusted myself off and wiped my hands on the front of my jeans. My tailbone hurt, my ankle ached and my head felt like it had been hit with a baseball bat.

As I rubbed my temples to clear the cobwebs, I spotted McKenzie Harper standing in the doorway peering at me. When Ms. Blabbermouth noticed I had seen her, she scurried into the room.

By the time I limped into social studies, my classmates knew about my run-in with Moose.

Fortunately, Mrs. Ward was late, so I didn't get in trouble for being tardy.

"Standing up to Moose took guts, Phil," CJ said as I hobbled passed him on the way to my desk. Classmates nodded in agreement.

"Harper flapping her gums again?" I asked.

"She didn't say a word. Didn't hafta. Moose and you were right outside the room."

"You okay?" Clara asked as I slowly eased into my desk across from her.

"Yeah, except for my head, ankle and tailbone. All three are throbbing."

"Your bottom lip is bleeding too."

I licked my lip. "Must've bit my lip while sliding along the floor."

Clara slid her hand into her jeans pocket and pulled out a crumpled tissue. "Here, use this."

I shook my head.

"It's not been used if that's what you're worried about." Clara set the tissue on my desk.

"Thanks." I picked up the tissue and pressed it against my lip.

"Tell Mrs. Ward what happened," Clara said. "Moose would get suspended."

"Leave it be," I whispered as if telling her a secret. "We only have two and a half weeks left of school. It would just cause me more grief."

Clara opened her mouth to say something, but Mrs. Ward rushed into the room. "Sorry, I'm late, class. I had to deal with an office emergency. Hope I didn't miss anything exciting."

Besides me being hurled down the hallway, no, nothing at all.

"No time for a joke today." The teacher picked up a thick book lying on the corner of her desk. "Please turn to page 186 in your textbook."

As Clara flipped through her textbook to find the page, she turned her head sideways and looked at me. "What you did, Phil, was amazing."

Taken aback by her compliment, I sat speechless. Beaming, I opened my book to page 186.

My lip bled the rest of the hour.

My headache remained the rest of the day.

My tailbone hurt the rest of the week.

Moose left me alone the rest of the year.

No one mentioned a word to me about the small crater I had put in the locker. By the end of the week, the dent had been pounded out.

A small crease was the only sign the locker had been damaged. But every time I walked by Locker 273, I glanced at the bottom of it. I was proud of that crease. It reminded me to never back down from a bully.

NEVER COUNT OUT
LADY LUCK

Some kids are born lucky. Take Shane. It's like he carries a four-leaf clover in his pocket.

He finds change in the coin return in vending machines, wins prizes at drawings and snags the bike rack's last spot.

Shane guesses right on multiple-choice questions when he hasn't a clue as to the answer. And if my friends and I compete against him in board games or at cards, we have a slim chance of winning.

Unlike Shane, I'm unlucky. Always have been.

At age four, Dad backed over my brand-new scooter

with his SUV. In kindergarten, I plugged up a toilet and flooded a school bathroom.

A year later, a custodian accidentally locked me in the school library. At my third-grade birthday party, my cousin's collie mistook my leg for a fire hydrant and peed on my tennis shoes.

When I was ten, I broke a bone in my foot jumping off a neighbor's tire swing. In fifth grade, I tripped over my skateboard, tumbled down the basement steps and suffered a concussion.

A number of misfortunes followed me to middle school. In sixth grade, I got soaked trying to skip English, a cheerleader barfed on me during lunch and my girlfriend dumped me for another guy.

Except for a cancellation of a skit I wanted no part of, my bad luck continued this year. I froze my toes during a fire drill, puked at a school dance and was tossed down a hallway by a bully. To top it off, I had to take Spanish.

For me, Spanish was like putting together a two-thousand-piece LEGO pirate ship with no instructions.

I had a difficult time pronouncing many of the words and only knew two-thirds of the vocabulary. I had a hard time counting to a hundred, reciting the days of the week or saying simple greetings.

I had failed half the tests, flunked five of eight quizzes and rarely earned above a D on any assignment. I had a D-minus average only because I handed in a ton of extra credit.

So I sat in Spanish with three days left of school, feeling sorry for myself. Oh, sure, I had crammed for the final exam the night before, but I doubted it would help.

How do you study for a Spanish final? You either know the language or you don't. A snowman at the equator had better odds of surviving than I did of passing the exam.

If I flunked the final, I failed the class. Flunking Spanish meant spending weekday mornings in summer school. While my friends slept in, goofed off and played video games, I'd be sitting in Spanish.

Even worse, every afternoon, I would be cooped up in my room studying.

I chewed on my thumbnail as Señora Garcia snatched a test from a pile on top of her desk. She snapped her fingers twice. "Chicos y chicas, eyeballs up."

Twenty-five students fixed their eyes on the teacher standing in the front center of the room.

Señora Garcia pushed her red-framed glasses up the bridge of her narrow nose. "I hope you brought at least one No. 2 pencil with a good eraser. If you didn't, I have some extra ones on my desk. Please grab a pencil now."

Ethan, a total space cadet, stood and plodded over

to the teacher's desk. He plucked a sharpened pencil from an oversized coffee mug and dawdled back to his seat.

As Ethan slipped into his desk, Señora Garcia said, "Do not write on the test. Any mark, no matter how small, will result in a reduction in your score."

Avery, who asked at least one question in every class, raised her hand.

"Yes, Avery?" the teacher said.

"How much?"

Señora Garcia flicked a strand of hair away from her face. "One point for each mark."

"What if I write on the test by accident?" asked Dan, his voice mimicking a dentist's drill.

"It will cost you a point, Dan."

The teacher held up a test so everyone could see it. She pointed to a twenty-two in the upper left-hand corner. "Your test number is found here. I'll explain this shortly." Señora Garcia paused for a long moment, making sure we all saw the number.

She put the test back on the stack, picked up an answer sheet and held it above her head. "Two quick points. First, fill in the entire oval. If you don't shade it in completely or make marks outside the oval, the scanner may count your answer as wrong."

"Second, after writing your name on the answer sheet, print your test number after your name. No name or number will mean a five-point deduction from your score. When done, place your exam and answer sheet on the cart in front of the room."

Señora Garcia picked up the tests and answer sheets from her desk. "Leave the test face down until I finish with directions." The teacher ambled over to my row and set a test and answer sheet on my desk.

I stared at the back of the test, knowing this was my last shot at passing Spanish. My hands began to sweat, beads of perspiration formed on my forehead and my heart raced. My mouth was so dry I couldn't move my tongue.

I bit my nails while Señora Garcia set a test and an answer key on each student's desk. After handing out the last test, she said, "The exam has twenty-five multiple choice questions."

I did the math in my head. Twenty-five questions meant each one was worth four points. Eighteen right gave me a seventy-two, a passing grade.

That's all I needed.

That's all I wanted.

That's all I hoped for.

As Señora Garcia marched down the aisle toward the front of the room, she continued giving directions. "Each question has five possible answers. Once you decide on your answer, carefully fill in the oval on your answer sheet."

She dumped the extra tests and answer sheets on her desk, picked up a black dry-erase marker and faced us. "Any final questions?"

Logan, who had the attention span of a mosquito, raised his hand.

"What is it, Logan?" Señora Garcia asked, folding her arms across her chest.

"What happens if we write on the test?"

Señora Garcia peered at Logan over the rim of her glasses and gave Logan her I-already-told-you-that-look. "I will deduct points from your score for each mark I find." The teacher's tone made it clear she was irked. "No more questions."

Señora Garcia glanced at her Fitbit. "You have thirty-nine minutes to complete the exam. Once done, if you have time, double-check your answers before handing in the test."

The teacher marched over to a whiteboard. "So you can pace yourself during the test, I'll have the minutes remaining in class on the board." She printed 39 on the center of it and set the marker on the tray.

Señora Garcia strolled over to her desk and stood behind it. "Turn over your test and begin. Write your name and the test number on your answer sheet right now so you don't forget."

I wiped my sweaty palms on my jeans and dug into my pants pocket for my good luck charm. I pulled out a rabbit's foot I had recently found on the playground and

laid the charm on my desk. If ever I needed luck, now was the time.

I flipped over the test and printed my name and 22 on the answer sheet. To get a sense of what I was up against, I skimmed the first two questions.

After reading the second question, I sighed. If all the questions were this hard, I had no chance of passing the exam.

I peeked at the whiteboard. It read 37, plenty of time to finish the test.

I reread the first question and shook my head. I mulled over the five choices, narrowed the answer to four possibilities and guessed. I shaded in oval C on the answer sheet.

I read the second question again, narrowed the answer to two choices and chose oval D. If most answers came down to two possibilities, I had a fighting chance of passing the final.

I nailed questions three, four and five.

I'm on a roll.

My good fortune was short-lived.

I had no clue as to the answers to question six and seven, so I used the "Eeny, meeny, miny, moe, catch a tiger by the toe" method to decide.

Questions eight and nine were no problem, and I was certain number ten was right. Fifteen questions left. I pressed on.

As I filled in the oval for question twenty, I felt confident I had eleven answers correct and had a good shot at two others. If I nailed the last five questions, I had a glimmer of hope of passing the final.

I glanced at the whiteboard. Six minutes remained in class. Time was no issue.

As I wiped sweat from my forehead with the back of my hand, I turned my attention to number twenty-one. I read the question but didn't have the slightest idea as to the answer.

Hello summer school.

I flipped over the answer sheet. I started to shade in oval A when I did a double take. I rubbed my eyes, leaned forward and closely examined the back of the answer sheet. My eyes almost popped out of their sockets.

I sat at my desk, stunned. Señora Garcia must've filled out the last five answers of her test key on top of my answer sheet.

She had pressed so hard on her pencil she had indented the ovals to questions twenty-one through twenty-five. The correct answers to the last five questions stared me in the face.

Or were they correct?

Maybe these were the answers to her second or third-hour's test.

Maybe the indentations were from a standardized test we had taken a month earlier.

Since I didn't even have a good guess as to the answer to question twenty-one, I had nothing to lose. I went with the indented oval.

I tried marking the answer, but my hands shook so much I couldn't fill in the oval. I closed my eyes and slowly counted to ten. I calmed down and focused on the task at hand.

Oval B blackened in.

I read the next question but didn't have the foggiest notion as to the answer. I shrugged and chose the indented oval. After reading question twenty-three, an uneasy feeling gnawed at the back of my mind. I sat back in the desk.

What I was doing?

I was cheating.

Should I tell Señora Garcia?

I nibbled on the eraser at the end of my pencil, debating with myself.

If I told her about the indentations, she would thank me for being honest, but I'd flunk the test. My parents would be hopping mad. They'd take away my phone and give me in-home detention at least through summer school.

Besides missing loads of fun, I might not pass the class. If I failed Spanish again, I would have to repeat Spanish in eighth grade.

I stared at the rabbit's foot and mulled over my dilemma. I decided my luck had finally changed. The indents were meant to be.

A wave of guilt passed through me as I filled in the ovals to the last three questions. I set my pencil on my desk and glanced at the Spanish wall clock above the classroom door.

With little time to review my answers, I hoisted my sweaty body out of the desk. I lumbered to the front of the room and placed my test and answer sheet on the metal cart.

While returning to my seat, the bell rang ending class. I stuffed the pencil and rabbit's foot into my pants pocket and grabbed my textbook. I joined my classmates as they streamed from the room.

Once in the packed hallway, pangs of guilt welled up inside me. I wheeled around and headed back into the classroom. "Señora Garcia, can I talk to you?" I asked while approaching her desk.

"Sure, Phil. What's on your mind?" The teacher quit writing something on an envelope, clicked her pen and set it on her desk.

I stopped in front of the teacher's desk and told her about the indentations on my answer sheet.

After explaining what I had done, Señora Garcia said, "Thanks for telling me, Phil. That took a great deal of courage. I know you need at least a D on the test to pass Spanish. Most students in your shoes wouldn't be so honest."

"You're welcome, Señora Garcia," I said and headed toward the door.

I stepped into the corridor with mixed emotions. On one hand, I felt good about telling Señora Garcia the truth. But I also had a sinking feeling in the pit of my stomach. I did the right thing, but I'd spend summer vacation retaking Spanish.

CJ was waiting for me next to a drinking fountain. "You headed back into the room. What gives?"

"Nothing," I said as we navigated our way through the hallway brimming with kids. "Forgot a pencil."

CJ bent down and retied his shoelace. "I expected the final to be harder. How didya do?"

"I don't know." I didn't want to tell CJ about the indentations on the answer sheet. "Hope I passed. It's gonna be close. How about you?"

"Got at least a B. If I guessed right on a couple of answers, I might pull an A."

"I'm sure you aced it." We stopped at my locker, and I entered the combination.

"Hope so, but I'll need a little luck."

I lifted the latch and yanked open the locker.

"Who ransacked your locker, Phil?"

"Whaddya talking about?"

"Your locker. It's a disaster, and I thought mine was bad."

"Who are you, my mother? Don't you hafta drop by the office?" I asked, eager to change the subject.

"Yeah. Why?"

"Well, you have less than two minutes to stop there and get to PE."

CJ glanced at the hallway clock. "Oh, great. Catch ya in gym."

"Gotcha," I said, ditching my Spanish textbook.

CJ took off like on some sort of mission.

I shut my locker, gave my lock a quick spin and headed to PE.

The following afternoon, butterflies fluttered in my stomach as I plodded into Spanish. I'd soon find out if I was spending the next six weeks having fun or attending summer school.

"Before we go over the test, I would like to mention two things," Señora Garcia said after the class had quieted down. "First, I enjoyed teaching you this year. Also, Spanish is an elective next year, so I hope you consider taking Spanish in eighth grade."

She has to be joking.

The teacher picked up a pile of answer sheets from her desk. "On the front side of the answer sheet is your test score and on the back is your semester grade."

Señora Garcia headed my way.

Chewing my bottom lip, I trembled in my seat like an out-of-balance washing machine as the teacher approached my desk.

"Nervous, Phil?"

"I'm fine, Señora Garcia." I cracked my knuckles.

Nervous? My whole summer, my whole life depended on passing Spanish. Nervous? I was a wreck.

While Señora Garcia thumbed through the answer sheets to find mine, I braced myself for bad news. She pulled my answer sheet from the pile and gave me a way-to-go smile.

As she placed the answer sheet on my desk, I noticed a seventy under my name. I couldn't believe it. I had passed the final.

Did that mean I had passed Spanish?

I flipped over the answer sheet. A red D-minus stared back at me with a brief note under the letter. "I did not count the last five questions. You had fourteen out of the first twenty questions correct, giving you a score of seventy. Congratulations on passing Spanish."

Written below the teacher's signature was: "Honesty is the best policy."

The grin on my face was bigger than an oversized cowboy hat. I had beaten the odds and passed Spanish. Lady Luck had come through.

As Señora Garcia went through the answers to the test questions with the class, I laced my fingers behind my head and leaned back in my desk. With my eyes half-closed, I daydreamed about summer vacation.

For the next half hour, I hardly heard a word the teacher said. When the bell rang ending sixth hour, my face split into a wide smile.

The school day was almost history and the last day of seventh grade would be a breeze. All I had to do in the morning was hand in my textbooks, listen to a short speech from each teacher and clean out my locker.

After lunch, I'd spend the afternoon getting classmates' signatures in my memory book.

I remained seated while classmates funneled from the room. After the room had emptied, I eased myself out of my desk, folded the answer sheet in half and tucked it in my back pocket.

I approached Señora Garcia, who stood alongside her desk. "Thank you," I told her.

"You're welcome, Phil. It's nice to hear a thank you from students. You made my day."

"Señora Garcia, you made my year." I walked out of the room with a bounce in my step and a huge smile on my face.

Summer, here I come.

I couldn't wait.

EPILOGUE

Despite many ups and downs, I survived my second year at Lost Creek Middle School. Seventh grade was like being a participant in a science experiment. Every day I made new discoveries, not only about school but about life.

I learned valuable lessons such as: It's important to stand up for yourself, never bet money you don't have and honesty is the best policy. I also discovered that one person can make a difference.

I had some great and not so great memories. I met the unforgettable Ellen, helped launch a successful schoolwide food drive and passed Spanish by the skin of my teeth.

I shudder when I think of freezing my feet during a fire drill, puking at a school dance and standing toe to toe with a school bully.

But most of all, I will treasure the times spent with my best friends: CJ, Shane and Clara.

I have no idea what will happen next year. Our group should remain intact, but I won't have Mr. Fry again. I had completed the school's health requirements.

As for Ms. Joyner, who knows. With my luck, she will probably move to eighth grade.

ABOUT THE AUTHOR

After a distinguished 34-year career, Phil retired as a middle school teacher from Ashwaubenon, Wisconsin. His ongoing passion for teaching and commitment to his profession, coupled with a unique ability to connect with students, earned him a Wisconsin Middle School Teacher of the year designation.

Phil's first novels, The Rules of Never and The Rules of Never: Year Two, chronicle the tribulations of students during their first two years of middle school.

Phil declines to comment on the extent to which either novel is based on his experiences as a teacher . . . or as a student.